S0-DPE-051

MYSTERY AT THE
SPANISH CASTLE

BOOKS BY RUTH NULTON MOORE

The Sara and Sam Series
Mystery of the Missing Stallions
Mystery of the Secret Code
Mystery of the Lost Heirloom
Mystery at Camp Ichthus
Ghost Town Mystery
Mystery at the Spanish Castle

Other Upper Elementary/Junior High Books
Christmas Surprise, The
Danger in the Pines
Ghost Bird Mystery, The
In Search of Liberty
Mystery at Indian Rocks
Mystery of the Lost Treasure
Peace Treaty
Sorrel Horse, The
Wilderness Journey

For Younger Readers
Tomás and the Talking Birds
Tomás y los Pájaros Parlantes (Spanish)

MYSTERY AT THE SPANISH CASTLE

Ruth Nulton Moore

Sara and Sam Series, Book 6

HERALD PRESS
Scottdale, Pennsylvania
Waterloo, Ontario

Library of Congress Cataloging-in-Publication Data

Moore, Ruth Nulton.
  Mystery at the Spanish Castle / Ruth Nulton Moore.
    p. cm. — (Sara and Sam series ; 6)
  Summary: While visiting relatives in Florida, teenage
twins Sara and Sam investigate a mystery on a nearby
key, where strange incidents are occurring in a villa left
abandoned by the death of a stage magician.
  ISBN 0-8361-3515-6 :
  [1. Twins—Fiction. 2. Florida—Fiction. 3. Mystery
and detective stories.] I. Title. II. Series: Moore, Ruth
Nulton. Sara and Sam series ; bk. 6.
PZ7.M7878Mxg   1990
[Fic]—dc20   89-29290
                                                  CIP
                                                   AC

MYSTERY AT THE SPANISH CASTLE
Copyright © 1990 by Herald Press, Scottdale, Pa. 15683
      Published simultaneously in Canada by Herald Press,
      Waterloo, Ont. N2L 6H7. All rights reserved.
Library of Congress Catalog Card Number: 89-29290
International Standard Book Number: 0-8361-3515-6
Printed in the United States of America
Cover art by Sibyl Graber Gerig

97 96 95 94 93 92 91 90 10 9 8 7 6 5 4 3 2 1

Contents

To April,
our young teenager,
with love

1

The Mysterious Light

SARA Harmon drew in a quick breath of surprise as she glimpsed the light shining from the small island across the bay.

There it was, gleaming at her from the tower room of the Spanish castle, like a fierce eye. All else was in darkness—the bay, the island, and the rest of the spooky-looking castle.

It must be very late at night, Sara thought. She could never sleep soundly her first night away from home. After tossing around in her bed for what seemed like hours, she had gotten up for a drink of water. Returning to her bedroom, she happened to glance out the window which faced the bay. It was then that she saw the mysterious light wavering back and forth at the top of the tower.

The Spanish castle was supposed to be empty, Sara thought as she kept staring at the strange light. Nobody had lived in it since the magician had died, and that was several years ago. Then why was a light shining from its tower window in the middle of the night? she wondered. Was the Spanish castle really haunted, as the kids in Bayport seemed to think?

Sara shook her head firmly. That was just kid talk. She and Sam didn't really believe in haunted houses. Just the same, she wished that Brian were here to see the light and explain what it meant.

*   *   *

From the time Sara and her twin brother, Sam, were able to travel alone, they had spent part of their summer vacations in Bayport, Florida, with Aunt Harriet and Uncle James Carson. Their white frame parsonage in the small gulf coast town was like a second home for Sara and Sam. And since Brian Hobbs, only a year older than the twins, lived right next door, the three of them had become the best of friends during those summer vacations.

Earlier that day, after Uncle James met Sara and Sam at the airport in Tampa, he dropped them off at the Bayport shopping center. He had urgent business with a member of his congregation and was already fifteen minutes late. The twins could easily walk across town from the shopping center.

As they were passing the familiar stores, they saw Brian. They waved eagerly as he came loping across the parking lot to meet them. Sara was about to rush up to their friend and throw her arms around his neck as she had done those other summers, but today she hung back, feeling strangely self-conscious. Brian seemed different this year.

For one thing he had grown a couple of inches taller, so that now he seemed to tower over Sara. He still had the spattering of freckles across his nose and his unruly thatch of blond hair, bleached almost white by the Florida sun, but he seemed older. He flashed Sara a shy grin as he reached for her suitcase. Other summers he would have let her carry it herself.

They passed a new food market on the next corner and Brian hailed an older boy who was lugging a crate of oranges into the market.

The boy smiled and called back, "Be seeing you soon, Brian."

"A new friend?" Sara asked, not remembering seeing the older boy before.

"Yeah. His name's Mike Terleski," Brian explained. "His dad owns that new grocery where Mike works part time. He and his family just moved here last fall, and Mike goes to high school at Coral Isle."

"That's where you went last year, wasn't it?" Sam asked.

Brian nodded, then went on to explain about his friend. "Mike's captain of the cross-country team this year, and he wants me to go out for cross-country and track. Man, can he run! He's the best cross-country runner in the school. Anyway, we've been working out together this summer. We try to run five miles twice a day."

"That's ten miles a day!" Sara exclaimed.

"Yeah, I know. It gets heavy sometimes," Brian

said, grinning down at her.

When they turned into the yard of the familiar parsonage, Aunt Harriet, round and rosy as ever in a pink pantsuit, rushed out to meet them. After she gave the twins a hug, she led the three of them to the picnic table under the jacaranda tree in the backyard and offered them cool glasses of punch and some of her homemade sugar cookies. She did most of the talking, asking about the twins' parents and marveling at how much they had grown since last summer.

Even though Sara and Sam were twins and shared the same auburn hair and hazel eyes, they were different in many ways. Sam was "the brain" of the family. As their mother often complained, he usually had his head stuck in a book and was worlds away. Sara was more interested in people than in books and had lots of friends. The twins had one thing in common, though. They both liked to solve mysteries, and with Sam's brain and Sara's uncanny knowledge of human nature, they were fairly good sleuths.

Aunt Harriet chattered on about the happenings at Bayport. Being a minister's wife, she knew just about everything that went on in the small town.

"The Chungs got here a week ago," she told Sara and Sam, nodding in the direction of the small cottage across the street that Professor Chung and his family had rented last summer. "Professor Chung is doing research again this year at the marine lab."

"Oh, great!" Sara exclaimed, remembering Lee-Ming, the Chung's pretty daughter, with whom they had made friends last summer.

"Lee-Ming has been asking about you two," Aunt

Harriet said. "I told her you'd be here today. But she and her mother had to go to Tampa to do some shopping. You can see her tomorrow."

Aunt Harriet picked up her palm leaf fan. "My, it is warm today." Her eyes twinkled as she turned to the twins. "I know what you're thinking. There's just time before supper for you three to go over to the key for a swim."

The twins nodded and looked eagerly at Brian. They had always shared his love for the little island across the bay. What fun they had had there other summers, gathering seashells, building sand sculptures, and exploring the grounds of the Spanish castle. They expected Brian to be as eager as they for a swim, but he hung back.

"Sorry," he said. "I promised Mike I'd go jogging when he finishes at the store." He glanced down at his wristwatch. "And that should be in about fifteen minutes."

Before they could express their disappointment, Brian turned quickly to Sam. "Ever think of going out for track and cross-country, Sam?"

Sam, the bookworm, grinned and shook his head. Sports had never been his thing.

"You're built like a runner," Brian persisted, sizing up Sam's tall, spare frame. "With a little training, I bet you'd be good."

"You think so?" Sam asked, excitement kindling his voice.

"Sure. Get into a pair of shorts and a T-shirt and join us."

"In this heat?" protested Aunt Harriet, fanning her red face vigorously.

Brian grinned. "Oh, Aunt Harriet"—he always called her Aunt Harriet—"it's a lot cooler on the key. That's why we run there."

With surprise Sara watched her twin grab the luggage and head for the parsonage.

"You and Sara can have the same rooms you had last year," Aunt Harriet said.

When Sam appeared a few minutes later, he was wearing shorts and a T-shirt. They didn't match at all, and Sara supposed that he had just grabbed the first pair of shorts and T-shirt he could find from the jumble of clothes he had thrown into his suitcase.

Anxious to be off, Brian shouted, "Come on, Sam. Let's go." Giving Sara a fleeting smile, he told her, "We'll go swimming tomorrow, Sara."

"I hope you two don't get sunstroke," Aunt Harriet called after them.

As they watched the boys' long-legged strides vanish around the corner of the house, Aunt Harriet shook her head. "Jogging, jogging, jogging! That's all Brian's interested in this summer."

"I can't see why he didn't invite me," Sara said, her voice tinged with disappointment. "Girls run cross-country, too."

For the first time since she had come to Bayport, Sara felt left out. Other summers it was always the three of them doing things together.

Aunt Harriet seemed to read Sara's thoughts. She looked at her niece with motherly concern. "Sometimes a year changes a person, Sara. All of a sudden Brian wants to be grown-up and doing things the older boys do." She paused with a wistful sigh. "It's too bad that things can't stay the same and that one has to grow up all of a sudden."

Sara looked intently at her aunt. Was Aunt Harriet trying to tell her, now that they were growing up, things could never be the same again?

"But I don't feel any different," she protested, "and I'm a year older."

Aunt Harriet reached over and patted Sara's hand with her plump one. "Some young people seem to grow up faster than others. I'm glad you haven't changed that much, dear."

Sara got up quickly to help her aunt take the empty glasses into the house. Then she went into her room to change into a cool pair of shorts and a blue pullover. As she brushed her hair, she studied her image in the mirror over the dressing table. With her wispy, auburn hair, her turned-up nose, and her pert chin, she supposed she hadn't changed all that much since last summer. Maybe next year she'd let her hair grow. Maybe then Brian would take notice of her.

With a sigh she picked up a paperback and spent the rest of the afternoon sitting under the jacaranda tree, waiting for Sam and Uncle James to come home.

* * *

Now at night, alone in her room, Sara looked once more at the strange light in the tower room of the Spanish castle. It wavered for a while, then suddenly disappeared. Mystified, Sara continued to stare into the darkness. It was not a ghostly happening, she kept telling herself. The castle was not really haunted. But what could that wavering light mean, shining from the tower room in the middle of the night?

Tomorrow she would tell Lee-Ming about it, she decided. Maybe they could walk over to the island

and find out what that strange light was all about.

Sara smiled in the dark. What was needed this summer to bring them all together again was a good mystery to solve. And maybe the mysterious light in the Spanish castle would turn out to be just that.

2

A Cabin Cruiser and a Haunted Castle

L EE-MING, whom they all called Lee, was wash-
ing the breakfast dishes when Sara knocked
on the screen door of the cottage the next morning.

"Sara!" she cried, running to the door. "Wow, am
I glad to see you! Your aunt said you were coming
yesterday. Sorry Mom and I had to go to Tampa and
I wasn't here."

"Oh, that's okay," Sara said as the girls threw
their arms around each other.

"Where is Sam?" Lee asked, glancing over Sara's
shoulder to see if her twin was there.

"Would you believe it?" Sara said, giving a little

laugh. "Sam's jogging on the island with Brian."

"I can believe it," Lee said with a sigh. "That's all Brian's been doing since we've been here. I've hardly seen him at all."

In a way Sara was glad she wasn't the only one Brian was neglecting. It was good that she and Lee had each other to chum around with this summer.

Lee was slim and pretty, with tilted eyes and long dark hair that bounced on her shoulders when she walked. Her face was a perfect oval, and the white shorts and green pullover accented her light olive complexion.

"So what's new?" she asked, plunging another cereal bowl into the sudsy water.

Sara had decided that she would save telling Lee about the light she had seen in the Spanish castle until they got to the island, so she simply answered, "I was wondering if you'd like to go for a swim."

"Sure," Lee replied eagerly. "I'll leave Mom a note. She went to the lab with Dad today." Lee's mother was a marine biologist in her own right and often spent the day helping Professor Chung with his work.

Sara reached for a dish towel above the sink and helped with the dishes. When they were all washed and dried, Lee wrote a quick note to her mother then went into her room to change into cutoff jeans and a swim top. Slipping a white headband around her hair, she called, "Okay! I'm ready."

Carrying beach towels and sunscreen lotion, the girls left the cottage door slamming behind them. At the end of the street they had to wait while the drawbridge opened its steel jaws to let a fishing boat through the channel of the bay. A flock of flapping, screaming gulls followed the wake of the boat as it pointed its prow toward the gulf. When the bridge closed again, the girls walked across it to the causeway, a thin strip of land that connected the island to the mainland.

Brian kept reminding them that the island was called a key. The word key came from the Spanish word *cay*, meaning low island, he had told them. The Gulf Coast was dotted with keys. Most of them were privately owned, like the Don Ramon Key. But since nobody lived there now they could use the key to swim and have fun on.

Sara knew that a famous magician, the Great Don Ramon, had owned the key. Uncle James had told her and Sam that before Don Ramon had died, he had written in his will that the key should never be sold to strangers. Since his only relative, a brother, lived on the West Coast, the Spanish castle remained empty all these years.

Mr. Herbert Thomas, Don Ramon's attorney in Bayport, was executor of the estate. Uncle James had persuaded Mr. Thomas to give the young people of Bayport permission to use the key for swimming and picnics, so long as they didn't litter or bother the castle.

There were no sheltering trees along the causeway, and the sun blazed down on the white shell road. Ahead, the sandy key, shimmering brightly in the heat, beckoned to the girls. Sara's heart quickened with happy anticipation as it always did when she first heard the gentle roar and splash of the surf and the laughing cries of the gulls.

When they reached the key, the girls left the road which led to the castle and scrambled to the top of a dune, scattering some sand sparrows from a clump of sea oats. Now they could see the blue-green waters of the Gulf of Mexico on the other side of the island. Several pelicans were bobbing up and down on the swells, looking over their ponderous beaks for fish. Little gray and white sandpipers were skittering back and forth along the foamy, white-edged breakers, as if they were afraid of getting their feet wet. At the far end of the key stood the tall white tower of the old lighthouse.

The gulf breezes wafted cool across their hot faces, and Sara filled her lungs with a breath of tangy salt air. It was just as she had remembered it from other summers.

"Come on!" Lee shouted, grabbing her hand.

The girls ran across the sugar-white sand and leaped into the breakers. With the first plunge they came up squealing with delight. The water near shore was as warm as bath water, but farther out cool, green swells curved over their shoulders.

They were both good swimmers and swam side by side until they reached the sandbar opposite the Spanish castle. It was then that Sara told Lee about the wavering light she had seen in the tower room the night before.

Lee brought a dripping hand out of the water to wipe long strands of hair from her eyes. "A light in the tower room?" she asked, frowning. "But the castle's supposed to be empty."

"Well, it wasn't last night," Sara said.

Puzzled, Lee stared across the water at the large pink mansion that commanded the center of the key. It was really fashioned after a Spanish villa, but everyone in Bayport called it the castle because of its square tower rising up in the middle. It was in the tower room at the top that Sara said she had seen the light.

"Maybe it was the ghost that everyone around here talks about," Lee said in a low, mysterious voice. Then she laughed, "Oh, really, Sara, you're putting me on. There couldn't have been a light in the tower. The castle has been empty for years."

"I know, but I did see—," Sara started to insist. She stopped suddenly when a movement on the beach caught their attention.

"Hey, there are Brian and Sam now, jogging along the shore," Lee said. "And another guy's with them. Hi!" she called, waving to the runners.

Brian kept running, and Sam followed several yards behind. The other boy, whom Sara recognized as Mike Terleski, paused and looked across the water at the two girls. Waving for Brian and Sam to follow, he splashed into the breakers and swam out to the sandbar.

"Hey, he's cute!" Lee giggled as the girls treaded water and watched Mike's long, smooth strokes.

"Hi there," he called, his face bobbing up to meet theirs. His wet dark hair was plastered against his tanned face and his tilted-tip nose and wide grin gave him a casual, friendly look.

Brian swam under water and came up alongside Mike. Puffing and splashing, Sam followed. Brian blinked the water from his eyes, slicked back his hair and his hands, and introduced Mike to the girls.

They goofed around for a while, ducking under the water and splashing one another until they were breathless. Swimming back to shore, they dried off on the beach towels.

After a while Mike said, "Let's jog back to the old lighthouse and take another look at the cabin cruiser."

"Okay," Brian agreed.

Sam turned to the girls. "We saw this neat cabin cruiser tied up to the pier while we were rounding the end of the key."

"Come on," Mike said. He started down the beach in a slow jog. An admiring Brian and Sam followed right behind him. The girls came splashing after them along the edge of the breakers.

When they reached the end of the key where the old lighthouse stood, they walked out on the fishing pier alongside it, and Mike pointed to the cabin cruiser docked inside the breakwater.

"It sure is neat," Lee observed. "Who does it belong to?"

Brian shrugged. "Nobody we know of. It has the name *Sea Breeze* painted on the hull, but that doesn't ring a bell either."

"Funny it's docked out here by the lighthouse all by itself," put in Sara.

"Maybe whoever owns it is on the key," Lee suggested.

Sam shook his head. "We haven't seen anyone while we were running, and we ran around the entire key twice."

Sara glanced up suddenly as the shadow of wings passed low over their heads and a long-legged bird came in for a perfect landing at the tide pool.

"Why, that's Charlie!" she exclaimed, remembering the blue heron they had tamed last summer with scraps of food. "Is he still hanging around here?"

Brian laughed. "Yeah, he's still begging for handouts."

The blue heron walked up to them on long, stilted legs. He stretched up his snaky neck and stared at them over a great pointed beak, waiting for a handout. When they offered no food, he made several low rasping noises, unfolded his enormous blue-gray wings, and flapped back over the sand to his tide pool.

Sam laughed. "He's telling us what a bunch of creeps we are, forgetting to bring food."

They stood looking at the *Sea Breeze* for a while longer, then sauntered back across the key. When they were opposite the Spanish castle, Lee stopped suddenly and announced, "Sara saw a light in the tower room last night."

Her words didn't seem to have much effect on Brian or Mike. Brian looked at Sara as if to say, you've got to be kidding! And it was obvious that Mike's thoughts were still on the cabin cruiser moored at the pier. Only Sam looked puzzled as he gazed at the Spanish castle that seemed as peaceful and empty as ever in the bright morning sunshine.

"Maybe the light you saw came from a boat out on the gulf," Sam suggested. "Or it could have been your imagination working overtime, Twinny."

"It didn't come from a boat," Sara insisted. "It came from that tower. And it was wavering back and forth as if somebody was carrying a light around in the tower room."

"But nobody's lived in the castle since the magician died," Brian protested.

Sara shook her head in desperation. "Why doesn't anyone believe me! I *did* see a light up there, and it wasn't my imagination working overtime, either."

They stood for a while looking up at the Spanish castle and its square pink tower. Finally Lee said,

"What's the story about the castle? I never did get it straight. Did a magician really live there?"

Brian nodded. "Yeah, the Great Don Ramon. He named the key after himself. Dad told me his full name was Don Ramon Montero. He came from Spain, made a fortune in this country as a famous magician, and built this Spanish villa here to remind him of his family home."

"Hey, that's something," Mike said, taking a sudden interest in what Brian was saying.

"When the Great Don Ramon wasn't all over the country performing," Brian went on, "he'd live here. But nobody in Bayport knew much about him because he kept to himself. Sara and Sam's uncle invited him to come to church, but he never did. In fact, during the last years of his life, Don Ramon lived like a hermit inside the castle."

"Why was that?" Lee asked, her eyes bright with interest.

As they strolled up to the gate of the Spanish castle, Brian replied, "Well, according to Luisa, his housekeeper, Don Ramon was in love with his pretty assistant, Clara DeLeon. When Clara left him to marry someone else, Don Ramon was so heartbroken that he gave up show business and lived here alone with his housekeeper. He shut himself off from even his family and friends."

"Oh!" murmured Lee. "How romantic and sad."

Mike leaned against the iron gate, hung between two stone posts, that opened into the driveway. He peered through the gate at the pink villa at the end of the drive.

"Go on, Brian," he prompted. "What finally happened to the magician?"

Brian took a deep breath and continued. "Well,

the story goes that Don Ramon became so obsessed with Clara's leaving him that he started to roam around the castle with that pet white rabbit of his, looking for her. Then one night while he was up in the tower room, Luisa heard a terrible cry. When she went to the tower to see what had happened, she found the magician's body at the bottom of the tower steps. The doctor said that Don Ramon had fallen down the steps and broken his neck. But Mom said he really died of a broken heart."

"Oh, how awful!" gasped Lee.

Sara nodded soberly. She and Sam had heard Aunt Harriet and Uncle James talking about this same tragedy. Uncle James had said that if Don Ramon had been a Christian, he wouldn't have been so lonely and heartbroken.

"When all others fail us, the Lord is there to comfort and sustain us," Uncle James had said.

Mike's voice broke through Sara's thoughts. "Why do the kids in Bayport think the castle's haunted?" he asked.

Brian frowned up at the villa, its shuttered windows like blind eyes staring back at them. "Well, one time some guys from town came over to the key to explore the castle. When they got inside and were walking down a dark hall, the figure of a man rose up before them. They scrammed and told everyone that they had seen the ghost of Don Ramon searching the castle for Clara. Nobody's fooled around inside the castle since then."

"Oh, wow!" murmured Lee.

Mike smiled thinly. "I don't dig ghosts. Have you ever been inside, Brian?"

Brian shook his head. "No way. Mr. Thomas told us kids that the castle is off limits."

Sam peered through the gate at the driveway that led from the castle to the causeway. It was lined with dark Australian pines, with ragged ribbons of Spanish moss draped over the boughs in ghostly garlands. It gave the drive a dark and spooky appearance.

Mike was saying, "I don't believe in trespassing, either, but if Sara saw a light in the tower room, maybe we should check it out. If someone's been prowling around up there, Mr. Thomas should know about it."

Sara's heart leaped. She could have given Mike a hug right then and there. She had always wanted to see what the inside of the castle looked like. If Mike thought they should check out the tower room, maybe Brian would go along with the idea.

But Brian hesitated. "You mean you take Sara's light seriously?"

"Sure, why not?" Mike replied. "Come on, let's see if there are any ghosts up there in the tower."

"Right," Sam agreed. "Let's explore." And with that he and Mike opened the gate and started boldly up the shadowy drive toward the Spanish castle.

Sara watched them go with rising excitement. There was a mystery to be solved here at the Spanish castle. She knew there was. And Sam thought so, too.

3

Ghostly Sounds

WHEN they reached the end of the drive, the Spanish castle rose up before them like something out of Disney World. Its stucco walls, once painted a bright pink, were now faded to a more subdued hue by the sun. A veranda, framed by lacy ironwork, ran across the entire front of the villa. There were little balconies by two upper windows facing the gulf. And up from the red-tile roof rose the pink tower with its four windows that overlooked the bay and the gulf.

Mike led the way up the wide stone steps to the veranda. Boldly he peered through one of the shuttered windows.

"Can you see anything?" Sara asked eagerly.

Mike shook his head. "The shutters are closed tight." He walked over to the big, carved front door and tugged at the brass handle. But as they expected, it was locked.

"I wonder how those guys from Bayport got in?" Sam mused. "You know, the kids who claimed they saw the ghost."

Brian shrugged. "Who knows. Maybe they got one of the shutters open and jimmied a window or something. Anyway," he said pointedly, "they weren't supposed to be here."

"Let's go around the back," Sara suggested quickly, not wanting to give up so soon. "Maybe we can get in that way."

"What good would that do?" Brian groaned. "The back door's locked, too."

Ignoring his words, Sara marched down the front steps and started toward the back of the castle. Sam joined her and the others followed.

Graceful palms and a pink-blooming mimosa tree grew alongside the villa. A walk of crushed shell led to a fountain where water once splashed upward. But now its tilted basin was filled with dead palm leaves and sand spiders.

When they reached the rear of the villa, they found the back door half hidden by clusters of sea grapes. Mike made his way past the sea grapes and tried the knob. To everyone's surprise, the door opened easily.

"This door should have been locked, too," Brian said, shaking his head in bewilderment. "Mr. Thomas is the only one in Bayport with the keys to the castle, and he always keeps it locked."

Sam ran his fingers along the hinges of the door,

studying them in his own deliberate way.

"These hinges have been oiled so that they won't squeak when the door is opened," he informed them. "Somebody must have been here recently." His hazel eyes met Sara's with a flash of excitement. The first clue?

Mike stepped through the doorway and looked around. The others hung back, their eyes wide and staring. But it was too tempting not to follow Mike inside.

They felt a pleasurable thrill of fear as they stepped across the threshold and into a long, dark hallway. It was like stepping into the haunted house at the amusement park at home, Sara thought. Only this was the real thing. She couldn't believe that they were actually inside the mysterious Spanish castle.

Everything was dim because of the shuttered windows, but by the bar of daylight from the open door, they could make out that the hall where they were standing ran through the middle of the house from the rear to the front.

"Come on," Sam said, his face breaking into a shadowy grin. "Let's explore!"

The five of them walked slowly down the dim hall. When they came to the first room to their right, Lee said, "Will you look at that!" She spoke softly. In the quiet of the empty villa, it seemed almost sacrilegious to speak louder than a whisper.

They followed Lee into a large room with two doors, one leading to the back hall and one to the front. The walls were wainscoted with wood panels, and a crystal chandelier hung from the ceiling. But the strangest thing of all was the platform, like a small stage, stretching across the inner wall of the room. On one side of the platform stood the shadowy form of an upright piano.

"This must be the performance room," Brian said with rising interest.

They looked curiously at him, then back at the room.

"I remember Dad telling Mom and me about this room," Brian went on. "Dad saw it one time when he came here to do some electrical work for Don Ramon. The magician told Dad that he had the stage built here so he and Clara could practice their magic acts. They used to entertain Don Ramon's out-of-town guests here, too."

"Wow, a little theater right in your own home!" exclaimed Lee.

They looked around the performance room a while longer, then Mike said impatiently, "Come on. We still have the rest of the castle to explore."

Across the hall from the performance room were two other rooms. Pale slits of light, leaking between the cracks in the wooden shutters, revealed a long table in the center of one, surrounded by fine carved chairs. An elaborate sideboard stood against the back wall.

"This must be the dining room," Lee observed.

"And the other room down the hall must be the parlor," Sara said, starting down the hallway toward the front of the castle.

Suddenly she stopped with a gasp, and Lee almost stumbled into her. Both girls let out a screech. There in the dim hall a dark figure loomed up before them.

They turned to run back to the open door, only to bump into the boys behind them.

"What is it?" Brian asked, looking over Lee's shoulder.

Sam moved cautiously past the girls. He reached out a hand to touch the dark figure. It felt hard and cold to his touch. It took Sam only a moment to realize that the solid figure standing in the gloom of the hall was not a ghost. It gave a clanking sound as he ran his fingers down over the helmet and visor to the breastplate, loin guards, and kneepieces.

"It's a suit of armor!" he exclaimed with surprise. "You know, like the knights wore in medieval times. Wish we had a flashlight to see it better."

"It sure looks spooky," Sara said, her voice trembling. "Wonder what it's doing here."

"Maybe Don Ramon used it in one of his magic acts," Sam suggested, "and when he gave up his magic, he put it here in his villa as an ornament."

"Do you think this is the dark figure those guys saw in the hall and thought was the magician's ghost?" Brian said with a half chuckle.

"Could be," Mike replied as he snapped his finger against the metal breastplate.

Lee took another look at the shadowy suit of armor, then whispered in a small, scared voice, "We have no right to be here. Let's get out!" But when the others continued down the hall, she quickly followed, not wanting to be alone with the formidable metal figure.

Just as Sara thought, the last door in the front hall led into the parlor. Lumpy shapes of chairs and sofas, covered with dust covers, filled the room. Sara paused in the doorway and strained her eyes to the far wall, where a large portrait hung. But it was too dark to make out the figure enclosed by the heavy gilt frame.

"Let's find the tower room," Sam said as he started up the wide staircase in the entrance hall.

The others followed. They discovered six bedrooms on the second floor and two bathrooms with old-fashioned tubs standing on clawed feet. All of the furniture was shrouded in dust covers which gleamed ghostly white.

"How do we get to the tower room?" Lee wondered after they had explored behind all the closed doors and found nothing but bedrooms, bathrooms, and linen closets.

The boys gave puzzled shrugs, but Sara had a sudden thought. She had noticed that one of the bedrooms in the center of the house was larger than the others, and they hadn't searched it as thoroughly. She turned and walked back along the hall. When she found the room again, she opened the shutters so she could see better. She guessed this must be the master bedroom, where Don Ramon had slept.

Glancing around, she discovered a sitting room attached to it. What a pleasant little nook, she thought as she stepped into it. It had two easy chairs hidden under dust covers and shelves of books that lined an inner wall. Between the shelves she glimpsed a narrow door.

Now where would a door like that lead to? Sara wondered. Another closet?

Curiously she opened it and drew back with surprise. For a moment she could do nothing but gape in astonishment at the square chamber with iron steps spiraling upward. Finding her voice at last, she called out to the others, "Hey, I think I found the way to the tower room."

While she waited for them, she stepped through the narrow doorway into the tower. Glancing down at the floor at the bottom of the steps, she caught her breath. She must be standing at that very same spot where Luisa had found the magician's body. She stepped back quickly as the others crowded around her.

When Sam saw the steps behind the door, he cried, "Way to go, Twinny! Let's start climbing."

They left the door to the sitting room open so that some daylight would brighten the dark tower. But even so, they had to go slowly up the narrow stairs, one halting step at a time.

Their footsteps echoed loudly in the hollow tower. It gave Sara the creeps. She was relieved when they finally reached the top and Mike pushed open the door to the tower room.

The room was filled with sunlight from the square windows on all four sides. Blinking to get their eyes adjusted to the brightness, they scrambled out of the dark stairwell, glad to see daylight again. Brian walked over to one of the windows to look out.

"Wow, what a view," he exclaimed. "Look at how far out on the gulf you can see!"

Sara peered out the window that faced the bay and Bayport, the window where she had seen the light last night. She gazed briefly at the view, then turned away. The tower room itself interested her more now than what lay outside.

It looked like a small attic, cluttered with all kinds of things. There were chests of various sizes, a long mirror, and a wardrobe. Next to the wardrobe was a folding screen, lacquered in red, with the name, THE GREAT DON RAMON, scrolled in silver.

"This must be where Don Ramon kept his props," Sara observed.

"Look at this," Mike said, bending over a screened, wooden box that looked like a rabbit hutch. "I suppose the magician kept his white rabbit in here."

Lee peered into one of the chests and drew out strings of colored scarves and silk flags. She dug deeper and found balls for juggling and at the very bottom a magic wand.

Sara opened the door to the wardrobe and exclaimed over the costumes that must have belonged to the magician and his assistant. Among them was a long, black cape with a red satin lining, the kind of cape she imagined a magician would wear.

She was about to point it out to the others when she heard Lee's voice pipe, "It looks just like a coffin!"

Sara shut the wardrobe door and turned to the center of the room where the others were standing around a velvet-draped table. On top of the table was a long black chest and next to it lay six shiny swords.

Brian was telling them, "I saw this trick once when the Great Don Ramon was performing over in Miami. It was called the Death Challenge. Dad took Mom and me over for the show. I was only a little kid then, but I sure remember it."

"How was it done?" asked Mike.

Brian studied the coffinlike chest. "Well, Clara DeLeon got into the coffin and Don Ramon closed it. He even locked it. Then he picked up these swords and thrust them through those slits you can see on the top. When he took out the swords again and opened the chest, out stepped Clara, unharmed."

Sam studied the slits. "They're real enough and so are the swords. When you saw the act, how did the assistant escape being stabbed when she was locked inside?"

"I don't know, but I'd sure like to find out." Brian tried the lid. It wasn't locked, and they held their breath as he drew it open.

"It's just an empty chest," Lee observed.

Sam stooped over to examine something. "Hello, what's this?"

He ran his hand along the inner side of the chest. There was a sudden clicking sound. To their surprise the bottom of the chest opened downward in the middle, revealing an empty dark space below.

"A false bottom!" breathed Brian. "So that's how Clara disappeared!"

While the others were examining the false bottom, Sara walked around the tower room to see if she could find a clue that someone had been in this room last night when she had seen the light.

If she could find something—anything that would prove to the others that the light she had seen had been real!

She looked at the other chests, the long mirror, and the folding screen. Finally her gaze rested on the wardrobe, and it was then that she saw the lantern.

It was lying right on top of the wardrobe in plain view. It was a battery lantern with a high-powered beam, just like one Uncle James kept in the garage for emergency lighting.

She should have noticed it when she was looking inside the wardrobe, but she had been too busy examining the costumes. Now she stared curiously at the lantern and wondered if it had really made the light she had seen from the tower room last night.

Of course! That's why the light was wavering. Someone was carrying this lantern while moving around the tower room. But who was that someone and what was he doing there?

She was about to walk over to the wardrobe to examine the lantern more closely when a sudden weird, unearthly sound filled the tower room. She stopped short and listened, her heart thumping in her chest.

At first the sound seemed far away, then it grew louder with strange vibrations, high-pitched then dropping very low. The next moment a man's muffled voice mumbled words she couldn't understand, followed by an eerie, faltering sound that rose to a high shrill cry.

The cry of a ghost?

Sam and the others stood speechless with fright as the mysterious sounds floated around them. It was Mike who found his voice first.

"Let's split!" he gasped.

They stumbled after him, out of the room and down the tower steps, the uncanny, haunting voice drifting after them—sounding like no human voice could ever sound.

4

View from the Lighthouse

AT the end of the driveway they stopped running to catch their breath. They looked at one another with wide, frightened eyes, then they looked back at the Spanish castle.

"What we heard up there—" gasped Mike, glancing up at the tower room. "I can't believe it! It sounded like something out of this world."

"It probably was," Lee said in a shaky voice. "It sounded just like I'd imagine a ghost would sound. And that horrible shriek at the end. Do you suppose that's the cry Luisa had heard when Don Ramon fell down those steps?"

Brian wrinkled his forehead, perplexed. "I don't

go for that ghost bit. What I would like to know is what *really* made those creepy sounds."

Sara had a sudden idea. "Could it have been one of Don Ramon's magic tricks?"

Sam's eyes brightened. He snapped his fingers and replied, "Yeah, maybe someone's hanging out in the castle and doesn't want anyone to know. So he scared us off with those weird sounds."

Mike shook his head. "That doesn't figure with the whole castle closed uptight and dust covers over all the furniture and everything."

"The castle sure doesn't look as if it's been lived in," Lee agreed.

"But the back door was unlocked," reasoned Sam, "and what about the light Sara saw in the tower room?"

His words reminded Sara of the battery lantern that she had seen on top of the wardrobe. In a hurried voice she told them about it.

Brian bit his lip thoughtfully and mused, "The lantern could have been left there by Don Ramon, but then the batteries in it would have been dead by now."

"You have to admit that something freaky is going on inside that castle," Sara said.

Brian nodded, frowning. "Yeah, but it beats me what it is."

"I think we should tell Mr. Thomas what we heard," declared Mike.

"I do, too," Lee agreed. "That's why we went into the castle in the first place, to find out about that light Sara saw and if anyone was prowling around in the tower room."

Brian thought for a moment, then shook his head. "Mr. Thomas would never believe the part about those weird sounds we heard. Let's keep everything to ourselves for the time being. We wouldn't want the reputation those other kids have of seeing or hearing a ghost."

Sam nodded. "I agree. Maybe we can figure out this mystery by ourselves."

Brian's eyes brightened with lively interest. "Sure, that's what we'll do. And if we can't figure out the mystery by ourselves, we can tell Mr. Thomas." He turned to the others. "How about you guys?"

"I think it would be kind of neat to try to solve it by ourselves," Lee said with a nervous giggle.

"Fine with me," Mike joined in.

Sara hugged herself with secret delight. Here was the mystery she had hoped for, and the others seemed as interested in unraveling it as she and Sam.

But as eager as they all were to discover what was going on in the tower room, they had no desire to return to the castle the very next day. So while the boys jogged on the beach the next morning, Sara and Lee spent their time looking for shells.

Brian had told them that if they found enough sand dollars, glossy cowries, and spiraled whelks, they could sell them to the shell shop in Bayport. That's how he earned the money for his running shoes.

The key was quiet under the warm summer sun. Even the gulls were silent. They were sleeping on the sand in even rows, their wings folded neatly against their sides, their bills tucked under their feathers. Only the gentle roar of the surf could be heard as the tide went out.

The Spanish castle looked as tranquil as the

sleeping gulls. It was hard to believe that just yesterday they had heard those spooky sounds in the tower room.

The girls searched for unusual shells among the piles that had been washed up by the tide. They waded out through the breakers and were lucky enough to find several perfect sand dollars. When their buckets were full, they trudged back over the causeway to Bayport.

They earned five dollars for their efforts and decided to go shelling again the next morning. After Mike left for work, Brian and Sam joined them.

"The sand dollars and the cowries sold best," Lee told the boys as they wandered along the surf, following the curving beach toward the old lighthouse.

"That's because they're the prettiest and the hardest shells to find," Brian said.

Charlie was not at the tide pool when they arrived at the lighthouse, but the *Sea Breeze* was still moored to the pier.

"You know," Brian mused, looking thoughtfully at the cabin cruiser, "the *Sea Breeze* has been here three days now, and we never see anyone on it or on the key."

"Strange!" murmured Lee. "Do you suppose whoever owns it is snorkeling?"

Brian shaded his eyes and looked out over the white-capped, blue water. "I don't see their snorkels. And if they were skin-diving from the boat, they'd be farther out in deeper water."

He glanced back at the landing. "I wonder if they could be some fishermen camping in the lighthouse. Dad says it's in good condition and perfectly safe to be in."

"Well, let's find out," Sam said.

As they walked across the pier, Lee looked up at the tall white tower and asked, "If it is in such good condition, why has the lighthouse been abandoned?"

Brian replied, "Because the coast guard now uses radar to guide boats around the shoals and reefs."

Brian had explored the lighthouse before, so he knew his way around. He pushed open the door, and they found themselves in a small, round kitchen.

"It doesn't look as if anyone's been camping here," observed Sara, glancing around at a dusty table, the rusty old stove, and empty shelves.

There were three floors above the kitchen. On each floor was a small round room with a window looking out over the gulf.

"These were the rooms where the keeper and his helpers slept," Brian informed them. But like the kitchen, the rooms looked deserted.

"Let's go all the way up to the beacon at the top," Sam suggested.

They continued up the long, winding steps until they reached the lookout and its large glass reflector. A walkway, like a tiny round porch, surrounded the beacon so that the lighthouse keeper could walk around and watch the gulf in all directions.

"What a view!" Lee exclaimed, her long hair blowing out in dark streamers in the stiff breeze. "You can almost see straight across the gulf to Corpus Christi, Texas."

"You can see the entire key from up here," Brian said. "Look, there's Charlie now."

They watched as the heron flew low over the water, then disappeared into the thick green foliage of the mangrove islands south of the key.

Brian grinned. "He probably has a girlfriend over there."

Sara made her way along the narrow walkway. Glancing up at the large reflector light, she wasn't watching where she was walking, stumbled over something, and almost fell. Catching hold of the rail, she looked down at a long leather strap that lay across the walkway. Her eyes followed the strap to a small black case lying underneath a wooden ledge.

"Look what I found," she called out. She reached under the ledge and brought out the case. Opening it, she drew out a pair of binoculars. She put them to her eyes and focused them on the key.

"Ah ha!" exclaimed Sam when he spied the binoculars. "Someone must be using this place for a lookout. I'll bet it's those people who own the *Sea Breeze*."

"Now who's letting his imagination work overtime!" Sara chided, a smug note creeping into her voice. "Probably they just brought them up here to see the view and forgot them."

Through the glasses the Spanish castle suddenly loomed into full view. Sara stood staring at the pink villa for a moment. Then she drew in a quick breath.

"There's a red car parked in the driveway of the castle!" she exclaimed.

She passed the binoculars around so they all could take a look. When Brian put them to his eyes, he cried out in surprise, "I see something else. Someone is coming down the walk by the fountain. He looks like a boy, but I don't think I ever saw him before."

Suddenly Brian tensed. His voice rose excitedly.

"Hey, he's climbing the steps. I think he's going into the castle!"

5

An Unpleasant Boy

SARA carefully slipped the binoculars back into the black case and put it underneath the ledge where she had found it. She quickly followed Lee and the boys down the winding steps of the lighthouse. Picking up their shell buckets, they headed across the key toward the castle.

When they came to the gate, Brian said, "Let's find out who that guy is and what he's doing here at the castle."

The open gate drew the four of them in like a magnet. When they came to the end of the drive, they stopped short. Someone was coming out of the castle. It was the boy they had seen through the binoculars.

They were near enough now to get a good look at him. He was about their age, with long dark hair framing a thin, angular face. He wore a blue tank top and cup-off jeans. He was frowning at them as he walked slowly down the stone steps.

The first thought that came to Sara's mind was that he was regarding them as trespassers. She felt a hot flush of embarrassment and wished that she could vanish quickly through the open gate. But with the others there, she had no choice but to go along with them to meet the unfriendly boy.

"Hi," Brian said, trying to make his voice sound casual. "You're new around here, aren't you?"

The boy jerked his head back to get the dark mane of hair out of his eyes. He made no reply.

Brian tried again. "My name's Brian Hobbs, and these are my friends, Sara and Sam Harmon and Lee Chung. Is that your car parked in front of the castle?"

The dark, sullen eyes peered at Brian from the boy's angular face. He ignored the question and countered, "So that's what you call it! The castle."

"Sure. Everyone in Bayport calls it that," Brian said matter-of-factly.

"I suppose they call it the *haunted* castle," the boy flung back, scowling deeply.

"Well, some do," Brian admitted with a little laugh.

The boy's frown tightened as he fastened his gaze upon them. "Well, it's not haunted," he retorted. "My mother and I are going to live here, and no-body's going to frighten us away. So beat it."

Sara stiffened at the boy's rude words. Lee stared uncomfortably, not knowing what to do or say next. Sam's ears were getting red, the way they always

43

did when he became angry. And Brian said, holding up his hands as if to ward off the boy's anger, "Okay, okay. Don't get all shook up. We're on our way."

They walked back along the driveway with deliberate slowness so as not to give the boy any ideas that he was chasing them off. Halfway down the drive, Sara slipped a glance over her shoulder and saw him still standing there watching them. She was surprised to see the anger gone from the boy's face, replaced by a curious, longing look—as if he didn't really want them to leave.

Brian was fuming. "Who does he think he is?"

"Well, for some reason he doesn't like us," Lee said in a puzzled tone.

"I think he insulted us because he thinks we're trying to frighten him and his mother away," Sara said frowning.

"That's stupid," Brian snapped. "Why would we want to scare them away? We're trying to solve the mystery at the Spanish castle, not cause one."

"But he doesn't know that," Sara replied in a low voice.

"Do you think he and his mother are really going to live in the castle?" Lee asked.

Sam shook his head, confused. "How can they? Uncle James said that Don Ramon never wanted the key or the castle sold to strangers. He left Mr. Thomas those instructions in his will."

"Well, you heard what that guy said," Brian mumbled crossly. "It looks as if Mr. Thomas sold the key and the castle anyway. And the way that kid sounded off, I have the feeling it's going to be just like the days when Don Ramon lived here, and nobody from Bayport was allowed on the key."

He shook his head and moaned, "Wait till Mike hears about this!"

* * *

That night at supper Sara and Sam told Aunt Harriet and Uncle James about the hostile boy they had met at the Spanish castle.

Uncle James leaned back in his chair thoughtfully. "I think I know who that boy is," he said. "I happened to meet Herb Thomas today. He told me the magician's sister-in-law came to his office for the key to the villa. He rode over to the villa with her and her son to open it up for them."

"The magician's sister-in-law!" Aunt Harriet spoke up with surprise. "But I thought Don Ramon's brother and his family were living in California."

Sam ignored Aunt Harriet's exclamation and broke in, "Then they are really going to live on the key?"

"I suppose so," replied Uncle James. "Herb said something about their inheriting the island and the villa. It seems that Don Ramon willed his entire estate to his brother and family. When the brother died suddenly this past year, his wife and son decided to move to Florida and live in the villa."

Aunt Harriet almost dropped the key lime pie she was serving for dessert. "Well, that's news!" she exclaimed.

Uncle James looked up from his iced tea and smiled. Like Aunt Harriet, he had a round, ruddy face and a short, plump frame. The twins always marveled at how much their aunt and uncle looked alike.

"For once I know something you don't know, Harriet," Uncle James said with a twinkle. "And that's saying a lot because you know just about everything that goes on around Bayport."

"I may know all that happens around here," Aunt Harriet told him righteously, "but I don't gossip. That's a sin."

Uncle James chuckled. "It is at that, my dear."

He turned serious once more and rubbed the bald spot on top of his head, the way he always did when he was puzzled about something. "I can't understand, though, why Don Ramon's nephew should act so unfriendly to you young people."

Sam frowned as a question hung in his mind. "And how did he know about the castle being haunted?"

"Oh, Sam, that's just talk," Aunt Harriet said as she passed the dessert.

Remembering what Brian had told them about keeping what they had heard in the tower room a secret, Sara darted a warning glance at her twin and quickly changed the subject.

"I suppose the youth group won't be able to have its annual cookout on the key this summer if somebody lives there now," she said. The youth group get-togethers at Uncle James' church were something Sara and Sam always liked to attend, and the annual cookout was the highlight of the summer. They always timed their vacations to include the cookout.

Uncle James leaned back in his chair and answered Sara with a suggestion. "Maybe Don Ramon's nephew is lonesome so far away from his home and friends. Maybe he would like to meet some young people at Bayport. He may even like to join our youth group."

Sam gave his head a definite shake. "He didn't act like it when we met him today."

For a time nobody spoke. At last, quoting from Proverbs, Uncle James said, " 'A man that has friends must show himself friendly.' "

Uncle James' eyes, serious but gentle, lingered on the faces of his niece and nephew. "I've often found that when persons seem angry with you and there is no reason why they should be, it is because something is troubling them. If you follow the Christian principle and take the first step in being friendly, you can often help them out of their troubles and at the same time make new friends."

Her uncle's words lingered in Sara's mind for the rest of the evening. As she got ready for bed, she thought once more about the unpleasant boy they had seen on the key that afternoon.

What did the boy mean when he had said that nobody was going to frighten him and his mother away from the castle? Had he, too, heard those frightening sounds in the tower room? Was that what was troubling him?

Remembering the longing look on the boy's face as he had watched them leave the castle that afternoon, Sara had the feeling that under the bristly exterior was a boy who was all alone and needed help. Maybe, as Uncle James had said, she and Sam could help him if they took the first step in being friendly.

She gave her pillow a brisk plump and lay back in bed. As she stared into the darkness, she came to a decision. Tomorrow she would ask Sam to return to the castle with her. They would go alone, without the others. Maybe if there were just the two of them and if the boy knew that they really wanted to be friends, he would talk to them.

She gave a sleepy sigh and closed her eyes. It was worth a try, anyway.

6

The Locked Door

SAM liked Sara's idea of visiting the boy at the castle. But it wasn't easy for the twins to slip off to the key by themselves the next day. In the morning Aunt Harriet asked Sam and Brian if they would paint the porch furniture, and Sara felt as though she should help. As a reward for their efforts, Aunt Harriet took them to the Pizza Palace for lunch, and Lee was invited.

It wasn't until the middle of the afternoon, when Brian left to cut a neighbor's lawn and Lee said she had to clean her room, that the twins were free to leave for the castle.

But when they reached the sandy key, Sam began

to regret their mission. The cool breezes off the gulf tempted him to run for the beach and into the surf instead of facing the disagreeable boy.

Turning quickly away from the inviting blue water, he resisted the temptation and followed Sara through the gate of the Spanish castle.

As they walked up the driveway underneath the shadowy pines, Sara's confidence began to ebb. The boy's dark, sullen face kept popping up in her mind, and she was remembering his angry words. But it was too late to turn back now. She and Sam were at the end of the drive and standing in front of the stone steps.

Sara took a deep breath and was about to follow Sam up the steps when a movement by the fountain caught her eye. Then she saw the boy. He was sitting on a stone bench under a palm tree, his elbows resting on his knees and his hands cradling his chin. He was staring grimly at the dry basin of the fountain.

Sara reached for Sam's arm and pointed in the direction of the fountain. Sam nodded and, bolstering their courage, the twins started slowly up the shell walk. The boy was too deep in his thoughts to notice them at first. It wasn't until Sara called out a cheerful, "Hi!" that he looked up with a start.

"Oh, it's you again!" He leaped up from the bench with fierce eyes and looked beyond the twins. "Where are your friends?"

Sara took another deep breath and replied, "You weren't exactly friendly yesterday. So it's only us today."

The dark brows drew down in the familiar scowl. "Yeah, well, why did you two come back?"

It was all Sam could do not to lose his temper

over the impossible boy. But remembering what Uncle James had said last night, he went on calmly, "We thought maybe you'd be lonesome here all by yourself. It must be strange living out on this key with no other kids around."

The boy regarded them suspiciously. "Do you live in Bayport?" he asked.

Sara nodded. "At the present time. But our real home is in Pennsylvania."

"We come here every summer to visit our aunt and uncle," Sam explained.

The boy blinked at them. Maybe the fact that they didn't really live in Bayport made his eyes seem more gentle. He slumped down on the bench and offered them seats next to him.

"What's your name?" Sam asked, this time with a warm grin.

"Andrés Montero," the boy told them, "but my friends in California call me Andy."

"Then we'll call you Andy, too," Sara said, heaving a silent sigh of relief that the boy was beginning to relax. "Are you and your mother really going to live here?"

Andy nodded. "Don Ramon was my uncle, and he willed us this villa and the island."

"That's wonderful," Sara returned.

"It would be if Dad were here, too." Andy's voice was tense again. "He died suddenly of a heart attack last winter, and Mom thought it would be better if we sold our house in California and moved here."

"I'm sorry about your dad," Sara said softly, "but don't you like living on the key? I think it would be fun."

The boy raised his shoulders and let them fall. "I

guess it'd be okay if someone wasn't trying to frighten us away."

The twins looked at him curiously. "Why do you think someone's trying to scare you and your mom away?" asked Sara.

Andy sat forward, his dark eyebrows drawn into a frowning line. "Because yesterday, while Mom drove Mr. Thomas back to Bayport and before I met you kids, I was exploring the tower. I thought the tower room would be a neat place for my bedroom, and Mom said I could sleep up there if I wanted to. Well, as I was climbing up to it, I heard these weird sounds. But I couldn't find out what caused them because the door to the tower room was locked."

"Locked?" Sam asked, surprised.

Andy nodded. "I didn't want to frighten Mom, so I didn't tell her about those eerie sounds I heard in the tower room. I told her I'd settle for the big room below it instead."

He looked unhappily at the pink mansion. "It sure would upset Mom if she thought someone was trying to frighten us away from the villa. She has her heart set on living here. She always talked so much about the Don Ramon Key, and now that it's ours, she's happier than I've seen her since Dad died. I guess the place reminds her of the happy times we three had here when we visited Uncle Ramon—that is, before he gave up his performing and wanted to live alone."

The twins looked at each other knowingly. Sara knew that Sam was thinking the same as she. Andy had confided in them, and it was only right that they should trust him. Anyway, it might help him to know that he wasn't the only one who was frightened away by those mysterious sounds.

First Sara told about the light in the tower room that she had seen the night they had arrived in Bayport. Then Sam told about the day he and Sara and their friends had explored the tower room and had heard those same spooky sounds that Andy had heard.

"It's strange about that door to the tower room being locked," Sam added. "It wasn't locked when we were there."

"Then that proves that someone must have been in the tower room and locked the door just before we came," Andy said. "That's all the more reason I believe someone in Bayport is trying to frighten us away from the Don Ramon Key. I guess that's why I made a scene yesterday when I thought all you kids came from Bayport."

"But why do you think anyone in Bayport would want to frighten you and your mother away?" Sara asked.

Andy shrugged. "For kicks, or maybe they resent strangers living on the key. Yesterday while Mom was in Mr. Thomas' office, I went next door to the drugstore to get a Coke. Some kids were there, and I saw one of them point to me and say, 'Is that the guy who's going to live in the haunted castle?' Then the other guys laughed as if it was some kind of joke."

Sam shook his head with understanding. "Now I know how you learned about the rumor of the castle being haunted. Some kids who live in Bayport did spread that story around, Andy. But it wasn't us. And we didn't cause the weird sounds in the tower room, either. They alarmed us as much as they did you."

Andy nodded. "I believe you now." Then he added

in a low, determined voice, "But I have to find out what's going on around here, especially for Mom's sake."

He looked so bewildered and unhappy that Sara spoke up, "We'll help you if you want us to, Andy."

"Sure, so will Brian and Lee and Mike," Sam added. He flashed Sara a crooked grin. "There's nothing Sara and I like better than solving a mystery."

Their friendly offer seemed to take Andy by surprise. He stared at them for a long moment, then his dark eyes softened, and for the first time he smiled.

"No kidding? You will?"

The twins nodded eagerly, thankful for Uncle James' Christian advice that was beginning to work wonders.

Sara beamed a smile back at the boy. When he wasn't angry or suspicious, Andy Montero was really nice, she decided. And not at all bad-looking when he smiled.

7

The Ghost
in the Tower

I'M not coming with you just because of that Andy Montero," Brian informed the twins and Lee as they walked across the causeway the next morning. "It's what he heard in the tower room that interests me."

Sara and Sam knew that Brian was still miffed at Andy.

"Oh, Brian," Sara said, "you'll like Andy once you get to know him. He acted unfriendly because he heard those same awful sounds we heard in the tower room and thought that we were trying to frighten him and his mother away from the castle."

"I guess I'd be upset, too, if I heard those sounds

in the house I was going to live in," Lee added.

"But why blame us?" argued Brian.

"Well, he said he overheard some kids in Bayport mention the *haunted* castle," Sam explained, "and that gave him the idea that some kids were trying to scare him and his mom away from the castle. For kicks, as he put it, or because they resented strangers living on the key."

"And since we were the only kids he saw on the key yesterday, he suspected us," Sara added.

Brian didn't reply as he grudgingly followed them across the causeway. Sara knew he was upset about the possibility, with the castle now occupied, that they wouldn't be able to use the key for swimming, jogging, or cookouts any more.

In silence they walked the rest of the way down the white shell road that led to the driveway. When they arrived at the castle door, a woman in a crisp, white apron answered their knock. Her brown braided hair was wound severely around her head, and her dark brows were frowning as she looked out at them.

"Who is it, Luisa?" asked a pleasant voice from the entrance hall beyond.

The woman turned and replied, "Two girls and two boys, Doña Dolores."

The next moment a small, pretty woman was at the door. She opened it wider for them to pass through.

"I am Dolores Montero, Andrés' mother," she said, smiling. "You must be the young people from Bayport. Andrés has been telling us about you."

"Yes, ma'am," Sara said, holding out the foil-wrapped pie Aunt Harriet had baked and sent along with them. "Our aunt thought you might like a key lime pie. They're awfully good."

"Why, how nice of her," Mrs. Montero said, taking the pie and handing it to the still-frowning woman by her side. "Let me introduce you to Luisa Garcia, who was Don Ramon's housekeeper. Luisa generously offered to come over from Miami to help us get settled. She knows the villa so well. Now let me see, your names are—" She stopped with a smile. "I believe you'll have to introduce yourselves."

Just then Andy came bounding down the stairs and helped with the names. He was all smiles today and seemed pleased to see them.

"Come, let's get acquainted," Mrs. Montero said, leading the young people into the parlor. "Luisa, could you bring us some lemonade, please?"

The sullen housekeeper nodded and disappeared down the hall toward the back of the house.

With the shutters open, the parlor was bright and cheerful this morning. There were bright-colored straw rugs on the floor, and the dust covers had been removed from the furniture, revealing a red velvet sofa, comfortable oval-backed chairs, and pedestal tables holding lamps and vases.

Here and there on the walls were hammered-copper relief sculptures and paintings of Spanish scenes. Sara walked over to the large portrait that commanded the far wall.

Now in the bright light from the open shutters, the portrait revealed the imposing figure of a man. A black cape lined with scarlet hung over his shoulders, just like the one Sara had seen in the wardrobe in the tower room. He had dark wavy hair, a small, pointed beard, and an aquiline nose. The portrait was so lifelike that the dark, deep-set eyes seemed to pierce right through her.

"That is a portrait of my brother-in-law, Don Ramon," Mrs. Montero said. "It was painted when he was at the height of his career. It is a very good likeness."

She gestured for them to be seated and sat next to Sara on the sofa.

Sara liked Andy's mother. She liked the way Mrs. Montero wore her silver-streaked hair in a soft bun on top of her head, with dark curly tendrils escaping around her ears and forehead. Her deep gray eyes and friendly smile made Sara feel comfortable.

"How nice that Andrés has found friends in Bayport so soon," Mrs. Montero said. "I was afraid that he might be lonely on the key with no close neighbors."

Andy fidgeted in his chair as he glanced over at the four young people with whom he had been so rude yesterday. But at Sara's warm, friendly grin, he relaxed and flashed her one of his quick, bright smiles.

Just then Luisa entered the room with their drinks. As she was passing the iced lemonade, Andy said, "Luisa, is there a key to the tower room? I'd like to take my friends up there to see the view."

For a brief moment the housekeeper seemed startled. Recovering her composure, she replied in a flat voice, "Don Ramon wanted the tower room to be kept locked after he gave up his performing. All his costumes and props are there and should not be disturbed."

Andy frowned down at his glass. They talked for a while longer, and when they had finished their lemonade, he said, "Come on. I'll show you my room."

They followed him into the hall where the wide staircase rose gracefully upward. But before they started up the steps, Sam said, "I'd like to see something first."

He walked down the hallway to the knight's armor. "This is really something," he remarked. "How old is it, and who was the knight who wore it? Some ancestor of yours, Andy?"

Andy laughed. "It's not a real suit of armor. Uncle Ramon had it specially made for his shows."

Sam lifted the visor and peered inside.

"Let me show something," Andy said, reaching around in back of the armor.

"Hey, it opens up!" exclaimed Sara.

"Step inside," invited Andy. "It was made large enough to hide a man. Uncle Ramon used it in one of his disappearing acts."

After they took turns stepping inside the suit of armor, Andy closed it with a clang, and they followed him up the stairs to the master bedroom. They made their way around some cartons in the middle of the floor that Andy had not yet unpacked. He led them to the little balcony to admire the view of the gulf. After that Andy gestured to the sitting room, where they sat on the floor and talked.

"Did you notice how strange Luisa acted when I asked her if there was a key to the tower room?" Andy said.

They all nodded. Lee said, "She doesn't seem exactly friendly."

"She's been acting that way ever since we came here," Andy replied with a frown, "as if she's protecting the villa from us. Mom says she was so devoted to Uncle Ramon that it's strange to her to have someone else living here. But I think Luisa doesn't really want us living here on the Don Ramon Key."

"Why not?" asked Sam. "She must know that your uncle left it to you in his will."

"That's another thing," Andy explained, giving them a concerned look. "Last night Mom told me that Uncle Ramon put in his will that we have to *live* in the villa to inherit it."

"But you haven't lived in it since your uncle died," Brian broke in, "and that was quite a while ago."

"I know," Andy said, nodding. "But the will doesn't specify *when* we have to live here—just that we have to. I suppose that we would eventually have come here to live. Mom liked the key and the villa, and Dad was always talking about selling his business and moving East."

Andy stopped talking and his face saddened. Sara knew it was because he was thinking about his father. He must miss him very much, she thought.

She shifted uneasily on the floor and tried to think of something to say. "Isn't it odd that your uncle wrote in his will that you have to live on the key to inherit it?" she asked.

"I asked Mom about that," Andy replied, "and she said Uncle Ramon put that provision in the will because he loved the villa and the key so much that he didn't want them sold to strangers. He wanted us to love them, too—enough to want to live here."

"That doesn't sound too far out," Lee spoke up. "But what does that have to do with Luisa not wanting you to live here?"

"Well, listen to this," Andy said, his voice tensing

as he continued. "If we don't want to live here, then the Don Ramon Key and villa go to Luisa, my uncle's 'faithful housekeeper and best friend'—to quote the will."

Sam looked up quickly. "Oh wow! Now I get it. Just you and your mom keep Luisa from inheriting the key and the castle herself."

Andy gave them a worried nod. "That's right. At first I thought that someone in Bayport, or you kids, were playing pranks on us because of the rumor that the villa was haunted," he admitted uncomfortably. "But now I believe it's Luisa who doesn't want us here. If she can make it so we wouldn't want to live at the Don Ramon, she'd inherit it all herself."

"Then you think she's responsible for those creepy sounds in the tower room?" asked Lee. "And that's why she didn't want you snooping around up there?"

Andy's mouth tightened, drawing his lips to a thin, hard line. "I sure do. Uncle Ramon's costumes and props that are stored up there are just an excuse for not giving me the key."

"The only thing is," Sara reminded him, "we heard those weird sounds in the tower room before you or Luisa came here to live."

Andy nodded knowingly, then went on to explain, "But Luisa knew when we were coming. Mom telephoned her from California to let her know what day we planned to be in Bayport. She has a key of her own to the villa and could easily have arrived here ahead of us to set things up."

"Yeah," Sam said, thoughtfully. "That would explain the light in the tower room the other night, the back door being unlocked, and the hinges—"

He stopped talking and caught his breath sharply. At that same moment they all heard the sound behind the narrow door leading to the tower. They looked at one another with surprise. Lee put a finger to her lips and whispered, "Listen!"

Four heads turned to the door as if jerked by a spring. From behind it had come the sound of another door opening.

"The door to the tower room!" Brian exclaimed in a hoarse whisper.

For a fleeting instant fear flashed across Andy's face. Then leaping to his feet, he flung open the door from the sitting room to the stairwell.

The others crowded around him in the doorway, blinking up at bright sunlight that spilled down the stairs from the top of the tower.

Sara caught her breath, her pulses quickening. The door to the tower room was wide open, and framed in the doorway stood the figure of a tall man with a black cape hanging over his shoulders. His head was flung back and he was laughing at them, his aquiline nose and pointed beard outlined sharply against the light of the room.

Andy let out a choked cry. "Uncle Ramon!"

They stood in shocked silence for a moment. Then, horrified, they stumbled back into the sitting room and slammed the door shut behind them. But they couldn't entirely shut out the man's low, muffled voice nor the cry of terror that followed.

8

The White Rabbit

ANDY leaned against the door, his face white, his brown eyes staring.

"Uncle Ramon!" he gasped. "It—it looked just like Uncle Ramon. But—but it can't be. Uncle Ramon is dead!"

They looked at one another with blank stares. Sara thought of the black cape, the aquiline nose, and the sharp pointed beard, just like the portrait in the parlor. An icy chill went through her.

"I don't get it," Brian was saying, shaking his head. "It's unreal—just unreal!"

"You can say that again," Lee agreed with a shiver. "Maybe we shouldn't blame Luisa after all. May-

63

be there is such a thing as a ghost around here."

Sam gave her a skeptical look. Now that the shock of seeing the phantom was over and the stair door was firmly shut behind them, he tried to think things out rationally. There had to be an explanation for that bizarre appearance. Spooky apparitions just don't happen like that to frighten people half out of their wits.

Andy must have been thinking along those same lines. He swung around and to their surprise he flung open the door to the stairwell. "I'm going up to that room and find out what's going on. This time I'm not running—no matter what!"

Brian looked at Andy as if he was seeing him in a new light. Sara knew that Brian had changed his mind about Andy when he called out, "Wait for me. I'll come with you."

"So will I," offered Sam.

The girls stood in the doorway and watched nervously as the boys started up the steep steps. The tower was dark now, the only light coming from the open door of the sitting room. The door at the top of the tower was closed. The ghost had disappeared.

Andy was the first to reach the tower room. He tried to open the door, but it was locked. He rattled the knob and threw his weight against it. But it wouldn't budge.

"Open up!" his angry voice echoed through the tower. But there was no answer.

"Let us try," Brian offered, but he and Sam couldn't force the door open either.

Andy plumped down on the top step and frowned back at the locked door. "If we could only get into that room, maybe we'd be able to find out a few things."

"What you need is the key," Sara called up from the bottom of the steps.

"But Luisa has that," Sam reminded her.

"Hey, wait a minute!" Andy leaped up and struck the heel of his hand against his forehead. "Why didn't I think of that before!" The next moment he was running down the tower steps, with Sam and Brian close behind him.

When they were all inside the sitting room again, Andy explained, "We don't have to ask Luisa for the key. Mom told me a duplicate set of keys to all the rooms in the villa is kept on a keyboard in the pantry. That one's probably there, too."

"Then why are we standing around!" exclaimed Brian. "Let's go down and get it."

"What if Luisa is in the kitchen?" considered Lee.

"I don't care," Andy flung back over his shoulder. "I'm going to get that key."

He led the way through the master bedroom and down the stairs to the hallway. At the far end of the hall, behind the dining room, he opened a door that led into the kitchen.

To their relief Luisa was nowhere in sight. They followed Andy into the pantry, a small dark room off the kitchen. Andy reached for a chain hanging from the ceiling, and a light flashed on.

"There it is," he said triumphantly, pointing to the wall opposite a shelf of canned goods where a board hung full of keys. Above each key was a small white card with the name of the room printed on it. Their eyes scanned the board, searching for the card that read Tower Room.

Sara's quick eyes spied it first. "Down there," she cried. With a shaky finger she pointed to a key at the bottom of the board.

Andy quickly slipped the key off the hook. He was about to drop it into his pocket when they heard a door open behind them. The next instant, hurried footsteps sounded across the kitchen floor. They swung around, startled, as they gazed into the angry face of the housekeeper.

Andy's hand closed tightly around the key.

"What are you doing in my pantry?" Luisa demanded, looking accusingly at the young people.

Sara hoped that none of them would give away their purpose by glancing back at the keyboard. But it wouldn't have mattered if one of them had. Luisa, herself, was staring at the empty hook at the bottom of the board. She turned to Andy and held out her hand.

"Give me the key, Andrés. I told you that your Uncle Ramon wanted the tower room to remain locked."

Andy opened his mouth to protest, but he stopped abruptly. With the housekeeper's formidable appearance and her stern words, his bravado vanished and he flushed a deep red as he handed over the key.

Luisa hung it back on the board and frowned darkly as she waited for them to leave the kitchen.

"Well, there goes our chance for searching the tower room," Lee said in a low voice as they were walking down the hall.

"Where'd she come from all of a sudden?" Sam wanted to know.

"From her room across from the kitchen," Andy muttered gloomily. "The door was shut when we entered the kitchen, so I thought she must be outside or somewhere else in the house."

Sara let out a long, deep sigh. "What'll we do now?"

But before anyone could answer, a loud crash, followed by a scream, sounded from the parlor.

"Now what?" Andy groaned.

They hurried in the direction of the sounds and almost collided with Mrs. Montero as she ran out of the parlor and into the hall.

"What's wrong, Mom?" cried Andy.

"Did you see it?" his mother gasped.

"See what?" they asked in one voice.

"A white rabbit," Mrs. Montero replied breathlessly. "It ran right into the parlor and knocked over that lovely Chinese vase. When I tried to catch it, it ran into the hall and I—I don't know where it went."

"A white rabbit!" exclaimed Andy. "What's a white rabbit doing here?"

"That's what I'd like to know," Mrs. Montero replied. "That vase was very rare. It was one of Ramon's most valued treasures. Help me catch that creature before it ruins anything else."

They scattered to hunt for the rabbit. The girls searched the dining room while the boys looked in the performance room.

"Maybe it went upstairs," Sara said after they had looked under the table and chairs and behind the sideboard.

"No, there it goes now," Lee exclaimed as something white streaked by the door and down the hall.

The girls hurried into the hall. "Now where is it?" Sara asked in dismay.

Slowly and quietly they walked down the long hallway. Lee stopped abruptly and held up her hand in warning. She stooped behind the knight's armor, and Sara heard her speaking a few soft, coaxing words. At the quiet sound of the girl's voice, the rabbit hopped right into her arms.

"We found it!" Sara called to the others.

The boys came out of the performance room and Mrs. Montero hurried from the opposite end of the hall. Holding the rabbit close to her, Lee walked with the others into the parlor, where Luisa was on her knees, sweeping up the broken pieces of vase.

"Hey, it's cute," said Andy, running a finger through the soft white fur. "And look at its big pink ears and eyes."

"It has a pink collar around its neck, too," Lee observed, "and there's a name on it." She squinted down at the collar. "Of course! The rabbit's name is Pinky."

"It must be someone's pet," Mrs. Montero said. "But how in the world did it get here in the villa?"

Luisa looked up from her dustpan, her black eyes staring at the rabbit. In one startled instant she was on her feet.

"Why, what's the matter, Luisa?" asked Mrs. Montero. "You look as if you've seen a ghost."

"Maybe I have," muttered the housekeeper. A shadow passed over her face as she explained, "Don Ramon had a white rabbit he used in his magic acts. It was called Pinky, too. It had a pink collar with its name on it—just like this one."

She paused, then in a trembling voice added, "But that was many years ago. That rabbit must be long gone by now."

At the housekeeper's words Lee gave a choked cry, and the rabbit leaped from her arms. It hopped across the room and disappeared again down the long hallway.

9

Aboard the
Sea Breeze

THEY searched a second time for the white rabbit, but this time, much to Mrs. Montero's despair, it had completely disappeared.

It was almost noon before they gave up the search. But before they left the castle, they promised Andy that they would be back the next day and would bring Mike with them.

After lunch Brian had more yard work to do and Sam offered to help him. Lee went with her mother to call on a friend, and since Sara was alone, Uncle James asked her if she would like to ride to Coral Isle with him on an errand for the church.

The ride along the gulf shore was beautiful, with

long beaches of white sand stretching down to blue, sparkling water. Uncle James was his usual jolly self, telling her interesting things about the places they passed. They rode along in silence for a while, then Uncle James asked how she and Sam were getting along with Andy Montero.

Sara told her uncle how they had taken his advice and had become friends with Andy. She told how Andy was afraid to trust them at first but how, after they had taken the first step in being friendly, he became friendly, too. Uncle James nodded and winked over at her with warm approval.

Sara was tempted to tell her uncle about the strange happenings at the Spanish castle that had been worrying Andy—those weird sounds in the tower room and the appearance of the ghost. What would Uncle James think about them? she wondered. But remembering what Andy had said about not wanting his mother to know of the strange occurrences in the tower room, Sara decided to keep quiet. Anyway, they had agreed to try to solve the mystery themselves.

On their way to the key the next morning, they filled Mike in on yesterday's adventure at the castle.

"So now we have a ghost in the tower and a white rabbit that pulls a disappearing act," Mike said.

Brian nodded. "And a creepy housekeeper who's been giving Andy a real hassle about the key to the tower room."

"I really blew it yesterday," wailed Lee, "letting that rabbit go as if it were a ghost or something."

"Well, Luisa seemed to think it was," Sara said. "Did you see the look on her face?"

"But it couldn't be!" cried Lee. "I could feel its little heart beat, and it was so soft and warm. Ghosts aren't soft and warm."

In the bright sunshine on the causeway, with the bay sparkling on either side of them, the uncanny happenings at the Spanish castle the day before seemed unreal. To Sara they seemed more like a wild, scary dream.

When they arrived at the villa, they were glad it was Mrs. Montero this time, and not Luisa, who met them at the door. Smiling a greeting, she told them, "Andy is fishing. He said I should tell you to meet him at the pier."

They thanked her and started across the key. As they rounded the curve in the beach and came within sight of the landing, Sam said, "There's Andy now."

"And there's Charlie with him," Sara added.

The boy and the heron had already made friends and were side by side at the end of the pier, both looking down at the water as if they hoped the fish would bite.

When they reached the pier, Sam called, "Hi, Andy."

The boy waved to them, and after introducing Mike, they sat along the edge of the pier, watching Andy's line and bobber as they talked.

"Anything new?" Sam asked. "Did you and your mom find the white rabbit?"

Andy shook his head. "Everything's been quiet, but we haven't found Pinky. That's what Luisa is calling the rabbit. She goes all over the house calling, 'Pinky, Pinky.' She's sure the rabbit is Uncle Ramon's white rabbit because of that collar it's wearing."

"Hmm—a ghost rabbit!" Mike mused. "that's a new twist."

Andy gave a bleak wisp of a smile, then changed the subject by nodding toward the cabin cruiser still docked alongside the pier. "Some boat over there. You guys know who it belongs to?"

"Nope," Brian spoke up. "It arrived here just before you and your mom came."

"And every time we see the *Sea Breeze*, it seems deserted," Mike added. "Like today."

Andy frowned thoughtfully at the cabin cruiser. "Mom said that boats are allowed to dock in the breakwater, but maybe we should try to find out whose boat it is since it has been here so long."

"Good idea," Mike agreed heartily. "Let's board her and find out. Now that you and your mom live here on the key, you have a right to know."

Andy reeled in his line. Taking the bait off his hook, he tossed it to the grateful Charlie. Then they all walked across the pier to get a closer look at the cabin cruiser.

Mike's eyes shone with eager curiosity as he and the boys stepped onto the deck. "Wow, what a boat!" he exclaimed.

"You better knock on the cabin door first and find out if anyone's there," Sara called out with uncertainty. She expected at any minute that the angry owner would fling open the cabin door and demand to know what the boys were doing, trespassing on his boat.

Mike moved over to the cabin door and rapped on it. They all waited anxiously. When there was no answer, he rapped again, this time more persistently. Still no answer.

"I don't think anyone is in the cabin," Andy said.

"Let's see if the door's unlocked."

Boldly he stepped up to the cabin door and turned the knob. The door opened easily. Seconds later the boys disappeared into the cabin.

"Come on; let's see what it's all about," Sara told Lee as together they stepped off the pier and onto the shiny gray deck of the *Sea Breeze.*

Sam appeared on deck and shook his head. "Nobody's in the cabin. Look for yourselves."

"It's really neat down there," Brian told them.

The girls stepped into a small galley and peered beyond it into an area that was used as sleeping quarters; only now the bunks were made up into cushioned sitting benches on either side of the cabin.

They looked around carefully but could not find any clue as to who owned the boat. There were no addressed letters on the foldout table, no books lying around with names in them, and they didn't think they should open the tiny cupboards to look inside.

In the pilothouse above the cabin, Mike was exclaiming over the wheel and the instrument panel. "This boat has everything. Ship-to-shore radio and even radar. I bet this cabin cruiser could cross the gulf. She looks seaworthy enough."

They looked around some more, then Lee said nervously, "Don't you think we better beat it before the owner comes back?"

Sara nodded agreement and joined her on deck. Hand in hand the girls stepped to the safety of the pier. The boys followed, with Mike trailing along behind. Mike was just leaving the deck when Sara caught her breath. Out of the corner of her eye she glimpsed a man and woman coming out of the lighthouse.

In one swift motion Mike leaped over the gunwale onto the pier. But not before the tall, dark-haired man and the woman by his side saw him.

"Hi," Mike said in a sheepish voice as the couple approached the boat. "Is this your cabin cruiser?"

The man nodded.

"I hope you don't mind if we looked her over. She sure is a beauty."

The man beamed at Mike's compliment. "Don't mind at all. We would have shown you around ourselves if we'd known you were interested. We were up in the lighthouse, enjoying the view."

Then Sara noticed the binocular case hanging over the man's shoulder. It looked like the same case whose strap she had tripped over the time they had climbed up to the light.

The man glanced up at the tall, white tower that loomed above them. "Remarkable old structure. They say its light could be seen for miles out on the gulf, but I guess with radar, there's not much use for old lighthouses like this one any more. I hope they never tear it down, though."

Brian spoke up quickly, "They won't. It's Bayport's one historic landmark, so it's safe."

"Good!" the man said, smiling broadly.

The woman had remained silent as she studied the six young people. Sara also did some observing. She noticed that the woman wore a pair of designer jeans and a cream-colored blouse. Her red hair was short in loose waves above her high forehead. Pale-blue earrings dangled gracefully from her ears. She raised a quizzical eyebrow as her blue-gray eyes swept from face to face.

"Are you young people from Bayport?" she asked.

"We come from there, except Andy," Brian spoke

74

up. "Andy here lives in the castle on the key."

"Castle?" the woman asked, turning to look back at the key.

"That's what everyone around here calls the villa," Andy explained.

The woman nodded slowly. "But we thought that the villa was empty. We were told that nobody lives here on the key."

"No one did until we moved here a few days ago," Andy said.

"What's it like, living in that big place?" the man broke in curiously.

Andy shrugged. "Okay, I guess."

The man held out a friendly hand. "We're Hank and Claire Cavanaugh. Since you live on the key, I hope we're not trespassing with our boat docked by the pier. You see, my wife and I collect rare shells, and the keys around here have the best shell beaches in Florida."

"Oh—oh, that's okay," Andy told them. "My mother said that the pier is public property. Everyone in Bayport uses it to fish from."

"It's funny we haven't seen you before," Sara spoke up, tilting her chin inquisitively at the tall stranger.

Hank Cavanaugh gave a quick laugh. "Oh, we're all over the place. We go shelling early in the morning and late in the afternoon. In the heat of the day we stay either in the *Sea Breeze* with the fan on or in the old lighthouse."

"How long will you be staying here?" asked Sam.

Claire Cavanaugh spoke up, "Just for a few more days, I'd say."

She gave them a little smile, then turned to the cabin cruiser. Hank followed her.

"Nice meeting you kids," he said, and with a nautical salute he stepped aboard the *Sea Breeze*.

They waved good-bye to the pair and walked slowly back to the beach.

"That Hank Cavanaugh seems like a nice guy," Mike said.

Andy nodded, but there was a puzzled expression on his face. "There's something about Mrs. Cavanaugh, though, that looks familiar—like I've seen her before, but I don't know when or where." He shrugged. "Oh well, I guess lots of people resemble each other."

Brian said with satisfaction, "Well, now we know who owns the cabin cruiser and why it's here."

"Yeah, that's one mystery solved," Sam added.

Mike stretched his arms lazily and said, "Guess I'll have to get back to Bayport. I'm helping Dad in the store this afternoon." He turned to Brian. "Is the youth group meeting at the church tonight?"

"Right," Brian answered. "You coming?"

"Sure thing," Mike said. "I wouldn't miss it." He shot a friendly glance in Andy's direction. "Hey, Andy, how about joining us?"

"Yeah," Brian chimed in. "How about it? Some of us kids in Bayport have this youth group at the church. We talk a lot, and if anybody is uptight about anything, we lend an ear and try to help out. We're all teenagers, except our adviser, Uncle James."

"But Pastor Carson is real neat," Lee said. "I joined the group last summer."

"The cookout on the key was a lot of fun last year," Sara hastened to add, hoping to entice Andy to join the group.

Andy looked down at the beach and scuffed up

some sand with his foot. "I don't know," he said evasively. "Mom and I don't go to church. I guess I'll pass on this one. But thanks anyway."

He swung around in the direction of the castle. "I have to go now. I promised Mom I'd help out with some work around the place." And without another word, he strode off across the beach.

"Well, how do you like that!" exclaimed Brian as they watched Andy disappear through the pines along the driveway. "You'd think, being new here and all, he'd want to meet kids his age and get acquainted."

"Maybe he doesn't dig church groups," Mike replied. "Especially since he said he and his mom don't go to church."

Sara had nothing to add to the conversation as they walked with Mike toward the causeway. She kept thinking about why Andy didn't want to join the youth group. Maybe it wasn't just because he and his mom didn't go to church. That wouldn't have made any difference anyway. Several kids belonged to the youth group whose parents didn't go to church. Maybe Andy was just shy, she thought. Or maybe he still didn't trust the kids at Bayport.

She let out a private sigh. Whatever the reason, she wished Andy would have accepted Mike and Brian's invitation. It would be so much more fun tonight, she thought, if Andy were there.

10
Andy's Urgent Call

THE youth group met in the all-purpose room of the church basement. Sara and Sam remembered how they had all pitched in last summer to make it into a real neat youth room. Even she and Sam had helped swing a paintbrush, transforming the drab tan walls into a bright blue color, like the hue of the gulf on a clear day.

The owner of a fishing boat had donated a net which was draped along one side of a wall. The kids had gathered sand dollars and starfish to add to the decoration. In Bayport the youth room in the church was the only real meeting place the teenagers could call their own, and they were proud of it.

Uncle James greeted everyone heartily at the beginning of each meeting and said a short prayer at the end. In between he sat in the back and just listened, letting the young people do most of the talking. He was a great adviser, they all thought. He was someone they could tell their troubles to, and he would understand.

Tonight the main topic of business was the annual cookout that was held on the key every summer.

Sara and Sam remembered how much fun it had been last year with everyone sitting around a bright driftwood fire. One of the boys in the group who could play a guitar had led the singing. A full moon had turned the sand to silver and brightened the breakers as they swept ashore, clutching at the beach with long white fingers of foam.

The twins, Brian, and Lee had sat together and shared in the singing. It had been an evening to remember, and Sara and Sam were looking forward to the cookout again this year.

But now Abby Mills, the tall, popular girl who was president of the youth group, was announcing that they would have to change the place of the cookout this year. A groan went around the room, and they all turned to Pastor Carson with concern on their faces.

Uncle James arose slowly from his chair, and the young people settled down to hear what he had to say.

"Don Ramon's sister-in-law, Mrs. Montero, and her son live on the key now," he told the group, "so it is no longer available for our cookouts. But we should be thankful that Mr. Thomas let us use the key as long as he did. We had many good times there, but we can still have those good times some-where else."

"But where?" appealed a girl sitting next to Sara.

"Well, Bayport has a nice little park along the bay," Abby suggested. "There are several grills there to cook on."

A loud protest went up from the group.

"Who wants to go to a crowded park with a lot of other people around?"

"We'd have to use those rusty old grills and couldn't have a beach fire or anything."

"Yeah, it was real neat on the key with a beach all to ourselves."

Abby held up her hand for silence, and when the protests settled down to a low grumble, she turned to Uncle James.

"As Abby said," Uncle James advised, "we'll have to go to the park. After all, there's a family living on the key now, and we just can't go over there with our crowd as we did other years." He paused with a shake of his head. "I'm sure your parents wouldn't welcome that in their backyards if they moved into a new neighborhood."

The grumbles grew fainter, and Abby quickly turned to the subject of food. "How about a clam-bake this year with all the fixings?" she suggested. "Mr. Salvos promised to donate the clams."

"Dad said if we're willing to pick out the corn and husk it ourselves, we can have all we want," Mike offered.

"And we can bring our own hamburgers and hot dogs," Brian added.

"Whoa!" Uncle James spoke up, laughing. "You kids are making me hungry."

So the meeting broke up with the youth group reluctantly agreeing to use the park along the bay for their cookout. Chairs were pushed into a circle and the talk session began. The girls had brought cookies and chips and the boys had furnished the soft drinks. Munching and sipping, they chatted until the food was gone and it was getting late. Then Uncle James ended the meeting with a prayer.

Sara and Sam had just made it back to the parsonage when it started to rain. It rained all night, and the next morning the sky was still layered with low, gray rain clouds.

Uncle James had an appointment in Tampa, and Aunt Harriet had a women's fellowship meeting at the church. From the living room window, Sara watched Brian and Sam jogging down the street in the rain. The house seemed empty—too empty, so Sara decided to go across the street to see what Lee was doing.

Lee greeted her with her usual enthusiasm. "Sara, am I glad to see you!" Then she added with a sigh, "There's nothing worse than a rainy day in Florida."

Sara laughed. "That's because it's not supposed to rain in the sunshine state."

The girls talked a while about the youth group meeting last night, then Lee brought out her backgammon board and they played. After a couple of games Sara saw Aunt Harriet dodging the raindrops as she hurried out of the church.

"Got to go now," she told Lee. "I promised to help Aunt Harriet make calamondin jam this afternoon. Someone from the church gave her a basket of fruit." She paused by the door. "Want to come and help?"

"Sure," Lee replied, her face smiling and eager.

The phone was ringing loudly when the girls entered the parsonage. Aunt Harriet was in Uncle James' study, answering it.

"It's for you, Sara," her aunt called.

"For me?" Sara asked with surprise. She couldn't imagine who would be calling her in Bayport. "Hello," she said tentatively, after taking the phone from her aunt.

At first the voice saying hi on the other end of the line didn't sound familiar. Then as it went on speaking, she recognized it and answered, "Oh, hi, Andy. What's up?"

"Can you come over to the key?" Andy asked. "I have something important to tell you." He added hopefully, "It's supposed to stop raining this afternoon."

"Oh," Sara moaned, "I promised Aunt Harriet that I'd help her make calamondin jam, and Lee's going to help, too. Can't you tell me now?"

There was a hesitation, then Andy said, "It's too involved to tell over the phone. How about first thing tomorrow?"

"That'd be okay." Before she hung up she asked in a low voice, "Does it have anything to do with you-know-what in the tower room?"

"It has plenty to do with the you-know-what in the tower room—and all over the villa," replied Andy, his voice sounding desperate. "See you tomorrow, then. And tell the others to come, too."

He hung up before Sara had the chance to say another word. Maybe he was afraid that his phone call would be overheard by Luisa. Sara remembered seeing a phone extension in the kitchen.

When Sam and Brian jogged back an hour later, the girls interrupted their jam-making to tell the boys the news of Andy's phone call.

Brian looked sulky and muttered, "I don't see why we have to go over there to help the Monteros when we can't use the key any more for our cook-outs."

"Isn't that being a little unchristian?" Lee flung back. "Anyway, maybe Andy and his mom will let us."

"Nah," grumbled Brian. "Not if Andy doesn't want to join the youth group."

"Youth group or not," Sara said, "Andy and his mom need our help. He wouldn't have called if they didn't."

"Okay, okay," Brian relented. "I'll call Mike, and we'll all go over to the key first thing tomorrow."

* * *

Andy was so eager to see them that he was wait-ing at the end of the causeway the next morning. They walked across the beach to the tide pool where Charlie flapped up to them, begging as usual for a handout. It was good they had remembered to bring some bread crusts with them. When the crusts were gone, the heron flapped away, satisfied, and they sat down on the sand to talk.

"Now tell us what this is all about," Sara said, impatient to hear what Andy had to say.

"Yeah, what's happening?" Lee asked. "Did you hear the weird sounds from the tower room again?"

"Not only that," replied Andy, "but we all saw the ghost of Uncle Ramon."

For a moment there was just the sound of the hollow roar of the surf and the pleading cries of the gulls. Then Sam broke the silence with, "How did *that* happen?"

Andy hunched over on the sand and fiddled with a shell. "Well," he began, "Mom, Luisa, and I were sitting in the parlor the night before last when we heard those creepy sounds from the tower room. Boy, they were really loud this time, loud enough to be heard in the parlor—all those odd vibrations and then that man's mumbo jumbo and that high shrill cry.

"Mom and I were starting up the stairs to investigate when Luisa screamed and pointed to the top of the steps. 'It's Don Ramon,' she said. Then Mom and I looked up and saw the ghost, dressed in that black cape, coming down the steps toward us.

"Luisa grabbed Mom and me, and we all ran back into the parlor. When Mom caught her breath, she said she was going to find out who that really was. She turned on all the hall lights, but nobody was there. It was as if the ghost had disappeared into thin air."

Sara felt goose bumps on her arms as she remembered the day they had seen the ghost in the tower room. How much more frightening to have seen it at night, with darkness all around!

"Did you see or hear anything else, Andy?" Sam was asking.

The boy nodded. "Last night we heard someone playing the piano in the performance room. But when we got there, the music had stopped and there was no one around."

Andy paused with a sigh. "Luisa remembered how Uncle Ramon liked to play the piano at night. She was so worked up that Mom had to make her a cup of warm milk and help her into bed. Then after she got Luisa settled, Mom wondered if she should call the police. But she decided that she'd sound pretty silly reporting a ghost, so we went to bed. But we didn't get much sleep."

"Do you think Luisa was faking it?" asked Brian. "You know, being scared and all?"

"She could have been, to get Mom all the more upset," Andy said. "Boy, this morning Mom almost freaked out when she found Uncle Ramon's magic wand lying on the hall table. Luisa said the ghost must have been prowling around the villa again last night and left it there."

"Oh, wow," breathed Lee.

"If all this keeps up, I'm afraid Mom'll really crack up and we'll have to leave the villa."

Andy looked so forlorn that Mike clapped his hand on the boy's shoulder. "Cheer up, old buddy. That's what we're here for, to help you find out about all the strange things that have been going on."

Sara blinked despairingly. "But how can we, now that they come at night? If there was only some way. . . ."

She stopped and stared at the bright expression on Andy's face. "What is it, Andy?" she asked.

"There is a way. You can all spend tonight at the villa."

At first they thought Andy was just joking until he explained, "Mom told me that I could have friends over to sleep in the villa anytime I wanted to. Tonight would be perfect."

He looked at them so appealingly that Sara burst out, "Oh, let's. I'm sure Aunt Harriet and Uncle James will say yes."

Brian twitched his shoulders. "Sure, I'll come."

Mike grinned. "If Brian and Sara and Sam aren't scared to sleep in a haunted castle, neither am I."

They all turned to Lee. At first she looked uncertain, then her face brightened. "Fine with me," she said. "I guess if all your parents say it's okay, mine will too."

"Great!" Andy said. "Let's go tell Mom."

When Mrs. Montero greeted them at the castle, she was smiling as usual. But Sara noticed that there were little worry lines on her face, and the shadows under her eyes gave away the fact that she hadn't been sleeping well.

Andy got right to the point and told his mother that he had invited his friends to spend the night at the castle.

When she looked concerned, he assured her, "It's all right, Mom. They know all about the strange things that have been happening around here."

"And you're not afraid of our ghost?" asked Mrs. Montero.

Sam flashed her a confident grin. "That's why Andy invited us tonight, Mrs. Montero. To help solve the mystery."

"And we'll bring our sleeping bags," Sara volunteered, "so we won't make extra work for Luisa."

"Well, if you are not afraid to spend a night in the villa, you are welcome," Mrs. Montero said with a smile of relief. "It will be good to have you young people to cheer us up tonight. How about coming early, and we'll have a picnic supper on the beach."

Later, as they walked across the key to the causeway and Sara thought about their commitment to spend a night at the Spanish castle, she felt a mixture of excitement and fear run through her.

"Do you suppose we'll see or hear anything spooky tonight?" she asked, looking back at the pink tower.

"I don't know," Sam answered. "But with all of us there, I hope the ghost does appear tonight. We won't be able to solve the mystery if it doesn't."

11

The Hidden Stairway

THE picnic supper on the beach was fun, even with the prospect of ghostly happenings that night hanging over them all. Mrs. Montero, despite her worries, seemed as cheerful as she had been the first time they met her. Even Andy seemed to be enjoying himself, and the rest of them certainly were.

"Mm—this fried chicken is yummy," Lee said as she took a bite out of a drumstick.

"Luisa's specialty," replied Mrs. Montero. "I'll pass on the compliment."

"The potato salad is Mom's specialty," Andy said. "Here, try some, Sara."

Sam, Brian, and Mike were too busy stuffing themselves with food to add much to the conversation. You'd think they hadn't eaten for a week, thought Sara.

When it was time for dessert and Mrs. Montero offered them thick slices of Luisa's chocolate cake, Sara groaned and said, "Oh, no thanks. I'm stuffed. If you don't mind, I'd like to have my dessert later."

She shook her head at Sam, who was digging into his slice of cake as if he hadn't eaten a thing before. "How do you do it?" she moaned.

Sam grinned. "Blame it on all the jogging I've been doing."

"I just have to get up and stretch," groaned Lee. She got to her feet and swung her arms around.

"How about a little Frisbee to burn off those extra calories?" Andy suggested, searching around the sand for the yellow disk.

They divided themselves into two teams, with Sam, Mike, and Lee on one team and Sara, Brian, and Andy on the other. For about half an hour they sailed the Frisbee back and forth. Mrs. Montero watched them for a while, then went up to the villa.

After each side won a game, they flopped down on the sand mats to rest. Andy held out a tidbit for Charlie, who had flown up from the tide pool to join their picnic. Sara turned around to watch them, and as she did so, she glimpsed a couple strolling along the surf.

"The Cavanaughs must be out shelling tonight," she said.

"They're not carrying buckets or anything for shells," Sam observed. "Maybe they're just taking a walk."

"You know, it's funny that they haven't come to the villa and introduced themselves to Mom," Andy mused as he watched the couple. "They seemed friendly enough the day we met them on the pier."

"Maybe they just don't want to bother your mom since they're not staying long," Lee reasoned. "Didn't Mrs. Cavanaugh say they'd be here just a few days?"

"Yeah, I guess so," Andy said, turning back to Charlie and feeding him the last potato chip on his plate.

As they watched the heron strut around searching for another handout, Mike laughed and said, "I hope old Charlie doesn't get sick with all the stuff we've been feeding him."

"Charlie get sick?" laughed Brian. "That bird has an endless stomach."

"Like you guys," Sara quipped, ducking a paper plate her twin sailed over at her.

After the blue heron flew back to his tide pool, they leaned against the side of a dune to watch the sunset.

"Gulf beach sunsets have got to be the most beautiful in the world," Lee murmured as they watched the setting sun fling long banners of red and gold across the sky, staining the waters a pretty turquoise, green, and red.

But sunsets in the semitropics do not last long. When the last bright color had faded from the sky, they gathered up the remains of their picnic and walked back to the castle in the purple dusk. Sara noticed that the Cavanaughs had not returned from their walk. But maybe they had strolled all the way around the key to get back to the *Sea Breeze*. It wasn't that far.

When they returned to the castle, they found Mrs. Montero in the kitchen with Luisa. Andy led the way upstairs to show them where to put their sleeping bags.

"I want you to see something," he told them after they had left their bags in their rooms and were following him down the hall to the master bedroom. He led them into the sitting room and picked up a long, slender rod lying on the bookshelf. "This is what Mom found on the table in the downstairs hallway this morning."

Sam's face sobered as he stared at the magician's wand. "You're sure it's the same one Don Ramon used in his magic shows?"

"We're sure," Andy replied. "We've seen it when we came here to visit and Uncle Ramon performed for us."

Lee examined the wand closely. "The last time I saw this was when I found it in the trunk in the tower room. How did it get in the downstairs hall?"

"That's what Mom and I would like to know," Andy replied, shaking his head. "Of course, Luisa thinks the ghost left it there."

As Sam watched Andy put the wand back on the shelf, he said in a determined voice, "I think we should make a plan of action, to catch the ghost if it should appear again tonight."

"Good idea," Brian agreed.

"What do you have in mind?" Andy asked eagerly.

"Well, we have to keep an eye on Luisa, for one thing," Sam said, "especially since you think she's behind all these weird happenings."

Andy nodded soberly. "She must know about Uncle Ramon's will if she was mentioned in it. She would know that she'd inherit the Don Ramon Key if Mom and I didn't want to live here."

"Okay, if anything should happen tonight, we have to find Luisa and stick with her to see what she's up to. I think Sara and Lee would be best for that."

"What about us guys?" asked Mike. "What can we do?"

"We'll tackle the ghost," Sam replied. "And, Andy, you better keep an eye on your mother so that nothing happens to her."

When they were finished discussing their plans, Sara stepped out on the little balcony. Now that darkness had come, the castle was beginning to give her the creeps. The big rooms were gloomy and full of shadows.

She leaned over the railing and drew in a breath of air, full of the heavy, sweet scent of night-blooming jasmine. The wind came up and rattled the palm fronds. It moaned through the Australian pines. Sara listened to the roar of the surf and the flight of gulls crossing low over the key, wheeling and calling.

And then she heard another sound. From somewhere high in the castle came the weird, unearthly strains, followed by the eerie cry.

"Oh no, not that again!" Sara cried as she fled back into the room with the others.

"That's just what we've been waiting for," Sam said, his voice shrill with excitement. "Come on, let's get going."

Andy handed Sam a flashlight, and Mike opened the door to the tower.

"Find Luisa," Sam flung back over his shoulder to the girls. "And stay with your mom, Andy."

Sara grabbed Lee's hand, and the girls fled down

the stairs with Andy following close behind. Mrs. Montero was standing at the foot of the stairs, looking up at them, her face pale.

"Mom, where's Luisa?" Andy asked breathlessly.

"Why, she's watching television in her room," Mrs. Montero answered. "What's happening up there?"

Leaving Andy to explain, the girls made their way down the back hall to the kitchen. The door to the housekeeper's room was open and the television set was on. But Luisa was not in her room nor anywhere around that they could see.

"Where can she be?" breathed Lee.

"That's a good question," Sara whispered back.

They peered into the pantry, but it, too, was empty. Their eyes flew to the bottom of the keyboard.

"There it is," Lee cried. "The key to the tower room."

"Grab it," Sara whispered urgently, "and let's get back to the tower."

Lee flipped the key off its hook, and they fled with it up the stairs to Andy's room.

The stairwell door hung open, and the uncanny sounds echoed louder than ever from the tower. At the top of the steps the girls could make out the dark shapes of the boys, Sam holding the flashlight with a shaky hand and Brian and Mike desperately trying to open the door. When they heard footsteps on the tower steps below, the boys swung around, their eyes wide with alarm.

"Phew," Brian said, wiping the sweat from his forehead with the back of his hand, "I thought you were the ghost coming up those stairs behind us."

"Where's Luisa?" demanded Sam.

"We couldn't find her, but we brought you this." Lee held up the key that glittered brightly as Sam beamed his light on it.

"Oh, great!" cried Mike. "That's just what we need."

He took the key and fumbled around the keyhole with it for several long seconds. Finally the key turned in the lock and the door swung open.

The tower room was dark. The beam of Sam's flashlight bounced around the shadowy corners. It raked the walls, then focused on a light switch just inside the door. Sam flicked the switch and a ceiling bulb flashed on.

Blinking in the sudden brightness of the room, Sara said, "That night when I saw the wavering beam, whoever was up here didn't use this ceiling light." She had to shout to be heard, for the distorted sounds echoed loudly all around them now.

"If he had," Sam shouted back, "the tower room would have been so bright that he could have been seen all over town. But by using the lantern, all you saw was its ray."

They stood looking around them, then Mike said over the din, "There's nobody but us here now. Where do those awful sounds come from?"

"Someone's been here recently," Sara observed, pointing to the wardrobe door that hung open.

"The door to the rabbit hutch is open, too," Lee said. But the hutch wasn't empty this time. There was a bowl of water, and next to it, a bowl of half-eaten rabbit food.

"So this was where Pinky disappeared to," Brian said, stopping to examine the hutch.

Sara walked to the wardrobe and began searching through the costumes.

"Just as I thought," she called to the others. "It's not here."

"What's not there?" asked Lee.

"The magician's black cape."

Just then Sam's frantic motioning drew them like a magnet to the lacquered, folding screen with Don Ramon's name painted on it. Sam was bending over something on the floor. When they gathered around him, he traced two thin wires that disappeared behind the screen.

Sara drew in her breath sharply as Mike and Brian pushed the screen aside. Concealed behind it were two blaring stereo speakers.

"So that's how it's done!" exclaimed Sam, leaning back on his heels and staring at the two speakers. "There must be a cassette player around here somewhere."

They didn't have far to look because the wires led from the lacquered screen to the big wardrobe next to it. Peering behind the wardrobe, they found the cassette player.

Mike fiddled with the switches, flicked one of them, and the cassette player clicked off. The silence that followed was like a breathless shock, and for the moment they just stood staring at the player.

Sam recovered first and bent over to take the cassette out of the machine. His eyes were round with excitement when he read what was printed on the side of the tape.

"Electronic music!"

"Electronic what?" asked Brian.

"Electronic music are sounds made by an electronic instrument called a synthesizer," Sam explained. "It creates weird pitches, vibrations, and distorted sound patterns. I found out about electronic music at the Record Mart at home while I was buying some cassettes for my stereo. The clerk played one of his tapes for me, and wow! did it sound far out. Just like this one."

He paused and clapped a hand to the side of his head. "I don't know why I didn't think of electronic music when we first heard these eerie sounds."

"But the man's mumbling voice and his cries?" Lee asked.

"That's done by recording a man's voice at different speeds," Sam said, "and those horrible cries can be done by distorting the sound of a raised voice electronically."

"So someone's been playing electronic music to make that ghastly noise in the tower," Sara concluded, flashing her twin a smile for being so brainy. "I wonder who he is?"

Lee glanced around the tower room. "Yeah, and how does the ghost, or whoever he is, get up here to play the cassette without being seen? Where is he now?"

"There must be another way into the tower than through Andy's room," Sam reasoned. "Let's take a look around. Maybe we can find where our spook is hiding."

Now that they had discovered the source of the strange sounds, the tower didn't seem so frightening, and they searched it with renewed vigor. With the flashlight they examined every inch of the walls at the bottom of the steps, but found that the only way into and out of the tower seemed to be through the door to Andy's sitting room. And the "ghost" couldn't very well have exited through Andy's room tonight with all of them there. Where did he disappear to after he had turned on the cassette player in the tower room?

Lee sank back against the wall and said, "Well, we found out all about the ghostly voices, but we haven't found the ghost himself. How did he get out of this tower without being seen?"

There was no answer to Lee's comment as they looked around the dim tower in bewilderment.

Sara was about to leave her searching behind the tower steps and follow the others into the sitting room when she tripped over a hard object on the floor.

"That's strange," she said out loud. She groped around in the dark until she felt the cold touch of metal. Tracing the metal with anxious fingers, she discovered it to be a large ring.

"I think I found something," she called out.

Lee and the boys rushed to her side.

"I'm glad you keep stumbling over things, Sara," Brian said, teasing her in a lighthearted way. He grabbed the flashlight from Sam. "Let's see what you found this time."

When he beamed the light on the metal ring tilted upright in the floor, he gave a startled exclamation. "A trapdoor! Right in back of the tower steps."

Handing the light to Sara, Brian pulled up on the ring. In seconds he had the trapdoor open, and they were gaping into a square opening where another pair of stairs plunged downward into darkness.

"Oh wow!" Sam's voice was excited. "We've been searching the walls for a door, never thinking that another way out of the tower could be a trapdoor in the floor. Nice going, Twinny."

"Let's find out where these steps lead," Brian said, and retrieving the flashlight from Sara, he led the way through the dark opening in the floor.

Sara's heart raced as she followed the others down the steep, winding steps. It was like climbing down into a dark pit, not knowing what was waiting for them at the bottom. At any moment she expected that they would encounter the hidden ghost. But when the steps ended and Brian swung the light around, they found themselves in a dark, square chamber with nothing but paneled walls around them.

"A dead end," groaned Lee. "Now where?"

"I don't know," replied Brian, flashing the beam of light over the walls. "There doesn't seem to be any way out of here but back up the steps."

"But these steps must lead somewhere," reasoned Sam.

They searched around the small square room at the bottom of the steps for another trapdoor in the floor, but they couldn't find any.

"Hmm," pondered Mike. "It sure beats me. Why would anyone build these steps that just come down to this place with blank walls?"

"Wait a sec," Sara said. "I have an idea. I've often read about secret panels that open in walls. Maybe there's one here."

The girls began to run their hands over the panels in front of them, and soon the boys were doing the same.

After several long minutes of pushing and shoving against the panels, Brian said with a groan, "It's hopeless, Sara. There's nothing here but solid walls."

"Yeah, and it's hot and stuffy in here," Mike said, wiping his face on his shirt sleeve. "Let's go back up."

But Sara was not willing to give up yet. There

had to be a reason why these steps had led to this small room. With a long sigh, she leaned her shoulder against the wall in back of her and tried to think of a reason why.

Suddenly there was a soft click. The next moment the panel she was leaning against slid sideways and she stumbled backward through the gap, almost falling into a room bright with lights.

Before the panel could slide shut again, Sam held it open while the others slipped through the narrow passage. With surprise they found themselves on the stage in the performance room. Standing by the piano, just as surprised as they, were the Monteros. Andy had the white rabbit cradled in his arms.

With a puzzled expression on her face, Mrs. Montero hurried over to them. "Where have you all come from?" she asked, mystified.

"The tower," Brian replied.

Mrs. Montero studied the paneling for a moment, then her eyes lighted up knowingly.

"So that's how Ramon performed his disappearing act for his guests!" she exclaimed. "Can you open that panel again?"

The panel had closed behind them, but it didn't take long to find the one Sara had leaned against. With the soft click of the hidden spring the section of paneling slid open, revealing the dark tower and the hidden stairway.

"That's just like Ramon, to build a secret panel and a hidden stairway in his villa," Mrs. Montero said, shaking her head. A thin smile curved her lips. "He used to love to mystify his guests with that vanishing act. But how did you find your way down here?"

Quickly they told how Sara had discovered the trapdoor behind the tower steps, and how they had found the speakers and the cassette player in the tower room. Sam had just finished telling about the electronic cassette tape when suddenly the white rabbit leaped from Andy's arms onto the piano bench. From the bench he hopped onto the keyboard, sounding a discord of notes as he ran across the keys. He seemed to be enjoying himself very much.

"Mom and I heard the piano while you guys were in the tower, and we found Pinky here," Andy explained.

"We still don't know where he came from, but he solved the mysterious piano playing that we heard last night," Mrs. Montero added.

"We know where he came from," Lee spoke up. "He's kept in a hutch up in the tower room, and someone must have let him loose tonight—and the other night, too."

"To frighten us again," Andy said grimly.

He reached out for the rabbit, but the creature wiggled his saucy pink nose at Andy and leaped from the boy's grasp. They all joined in the chase as he hopped across the performance hall and out the door.

"Down the hallway," Andy shouted. "He's heading for the stairs."

Andy turned quickly and ran after the rabbit. At the bottom of the stairway, he skidded to a stop and sucked in his breath with surprise.

"Look!" he gasped.

When the others joined him, their eyes followed his pointing finger. Forgetting about the white rabbit that had disappeared up the steps, they stared in horror at what Andy was pointing to.

Standing at the top of the stairway, with the upper hall light shining down on him, was the figure of a tall man dressed in a black cape lined with scarlet. He was looking down over an aquiline nose and a sharply pointed beard.

The ghost of Don Ramon!

12

The Ghost Explains

FROM the top of the stairs, Luisa was leaned over the banister and with a shaking hand, pointed at the ghostly figure that had slowly started to descend the stairs.

"It—it's Don Ramon!" she warned. "He's coming down the steps!" With a terrifying cry, she ran back into the upper hallway.

For a brief moment everyone was too shaken to speak or move. Then, as if Luisa's voice triggered them into action, the four boys sprang up the stairs, taking the steps two at a time. The startled ghost faltered, then swung around and fled back to the upper hall, the boys right on his heels.

Instantly there were sounds of a scuffle, accompanied by another one of Luisa's cries. Sara bit her lip and clasped her hands together tightly. She wished there were something she could do to help, but Mrs. Montero held the two girls close to her, with trembling arms around both of them.

After another long moment of suspense, they heard a man's voice call out, "Okay—I give up!" And a minute later the boys were escorting a disheveled "ghost" down the long stairway.

"Look who we have here!" Andy called out, waving a face mask for them to see. Brian and Mike followed, escorting a tall man between them. Sam brought up the rear, a satisfied grin on his face.

Sara's mouth fell open as she stared up at the man. "Hank Cavanaugh!" she gasped.

Now that the ghost was unmasked and her fear was gone, Luisa followed the others downstairs. She shook her head with disapproval as she stared at the man. "No, without the mask he is Enrique Cavallo, and I'd like to know what he's doing in this house, frightening us half to death."

Andy jerked his head around to get a better look at their specter. "Why did you call him Enrique Cavallo, Luisa? His name is Hank Cavanaugh."

The housekeeper gave the man a long, hard look. "Hank Cavanaugh is probably a name he dreamed up to call himself so that nobody would know who he really is. But he's Enrique Cavallo, Clara DeLeon's husband. You never met him, Andrés, but I did when he came to the villa to make masks for Don Ramon to wear for his performances. He's quite an expert."

"He sure is," grinned Andy, holding out the face mask and insisting that Enrique Cavallo—alias

Hank Cavanaugh—put it on.

The frightened ghost once more became the amiable owner of the cabin cruiser. As if it were just one big joke, he gave a hollow laugh and slipped on the mask.

Staring at Enrique Cavallo, wearing the magician's cape and with the mask covering his face, they could scarcely believe their eyes. He looked just like the portrait of Don Ramon in the parlor. As Luisa had said, Enrique was certainly an expert mask maker.

All this time Mrs. Montero had been listening in silence. Now she spoke, and her voice had an icy edge to it. "Mr. Cavallo, I believe you have some explaining to do. We may as well go into the parlor and be comfortable while you tell us what all this is about."

At her words, Enrique Cavallo darted a quick glance at the front door. He made a sudden side step toward it, but the boys quickly blocked his way.

Enrique twitched his shoulders in a gesture of resignation. Defeat shone in his dark eyes.

"Okay, okay," he said, shaking his head. "Just let me leave here after I explain."

"We will be glad to have you leave here after you explain," Mrs. Montero said crisply.

Enrique followed her into the parlor and sank heavily into the chair she pointed out for him. His eyes went narrow as he glanced around the room.

"Where is Clara?" he asked, to everyone's surprise. "She wanted me to do all this. It was her idea, not mine. She should be the one to do the explaining."

Mrs. Montero stared at the man with astonishment. "Do you mean that Clara is here, too?"

"You bet she is," Enrique replied with a harsh laugh. "She's here somewhere. She knows the inside of this villa like the back of her hand."

"I know," Luisa returned bitterly. "Clara has stayed here many times. Don Ramon wanted to make her mistress of this house, but she broke his heart when she left to marry you, Enrique."

Andy's impatient voice broke in at that moment. "Quit stalling, Mr. Cavallo." Glowering at the impostor, he prompted, "Go on. Like my mother said, tell us why you came here to frighten us."

Enrique ran his fingers through his tousled hair, took a deep breath, then launched into his story.

"Okay, it was like this," he said roughly. "After we were married, Clara talked me into going to Mexico to live, so we headed for Monterrey. There we met a wealthy man who made his money by smuggling ancient art objects out of Mexico to be sold to art collectors in the United States and other countries. He asked us if we would help him and offered to pay us handsomely if we did.

"It all seemed simple enough. We were to station ourselves on the gulf coast near Tampa and wait for a cabin cruiser carrying the art objects. We had to be where we could see the boat's signal in the night and where we could signal back that we were coming in the *Sea Breeze* to pick up the stolen stuff.

"Right away Clara thought of the Don Ramon Key and the tower room in the villa. She knew about Don Ramon's death and that the empty villa was locked up and off limits to everyone. The tower room would be a perfect place to watch for the Mexican cabin cruiser and to signal to it."

Enrique paused for breath, then went on. "When we came to the key, we decided to tie up at the pier and act like shell collectors. Clara suggested that we keep our eye on the villa for a couple of days to be sure it was safe to come here. From the top of the lighthouse, we could see the entire key."

"Then it was your binoculars hidden by the walkway under the reflector light," Sara broke in. She went on quickly, "And I suppose that lantern on top of the wardrobe in the tower room was yours, too."

Enrique nodded and shifted uneasily in his chair. "The boat from Mexico is to be here sometime this week. We were to watch for it each night. When it arrived, it was to signal to us and we were to flash back with the high-powered beam of the lantern. Then we were to meet the cabin cruiser in the *Sea Breeze*, pick up the art objects, and hide them here in the villa until we could get them safely to Tampa."

The five young people looked at one another knowingly.

"So it was *your* light that Sara saw in the tower room the night she arrived at Bayport," Lee spoke up.

"If it weren't for Sara seeing that light," Brian said, "we wouldn't have explored the villa the next day. You must have been in the tower room that day, too, Mr. Cavallo."

With a sigh Enrique nodded again. "Clara and I were there to set things up. We had to duck behind the wardrobe when you kids arrived. Boy, what a surprise you gave us, popping up out of the blue like that! It was too late to think of another place to signal and to store the stolen art objects. The lighthouse is too public, so we had to go through with the plan to signal from here."

"That's why the door to the tower room was unlocked that day," Sam said.

"That's right," Enrique replied. "Clara still has her own keys to the villa and to the tower room where all her costumes are kept, but we made sure the door to the tower room was kept locked after that. Only Clara forgot about the spare keys kept on the panel in the pantry. Were we surprised that you kids could get into the tower room tonight!"

"About the weird sounds we heard," Sam mentioned. "You and Clara must have played the cassette player we found behind the wardrobe."

Enrique nodded. "That first day when we saw you kids enter the villa and heard you exploring around we had to do some quick thinking to get you out of here. We found the magician's cassette player behind the wardrobe and a cassette that he used for one of his acts."

Enrique laughed in spite of himself. "When Clara played the tape, those bizarre sounds sent chills even up my spine. And did you kids scram from that tower room in a hurry! We thought you'd be so scared you'd never come back."

Andy ignored the man's mocking laugh and countered with, "Well, I guess we surprised you, too, Mr. Cavallo, when my mother, Luisa, and I came here to live."

"Did you!" exclaimed Enrique. "The villa had been empty for a long time, then this week of all weeks you had to come here to live. I was for calling the whole thing off, but Clara reminded me of all the money that was coming to us if we pulled off the job. So I gave in, and she devised a plan to frighten you away.

"She had heard the rumor that some kids in Bayport had spread around about the castle being haunted, so she thought up the scheme of getting me to disguise myself as the Great Don Ramon and to appear on the tower steps. We thought that if we could frighten you away so that you'd go into town for a while, we'd be able to pick up the art objects and then get away. When you, Mrs. Montero, found Don Ramon's wand on the hall table this morning, we were sure that we had frightened you enough to leave."

"How did Clara know that Doña Dolores would not have called the police?" Luisa asked.

Enrique's mouth twisted into a crooked smile. "Oh, Clara gambled on Mrs. Montero thinking it would sound silly to report a ghost."

"And I did think that," Andy's mother admitted.

"The white rabbit," Andy wanted to know. "Was that part of your act to frighten us away?"

Enrique Cavallo, still smiling, leaned forward in his chair. "When Clara found Pinky's old collar in the tower room, she thought that Don Ramon's white rabbit would give Luisa a good scare. So she bought a rabbit at a pet shop and put the collar on it."

Luisa looked indignant, but before she could say anything, Sam interjected, "Then you must have used the secret panel in the performance room, Mr. Cavallo. I suppose that's how Pinky got onto the stage and how you and Clara got in and out of the castle and into the tower room without being seen."

Enrique leaned back in his chair and studied the four young people with narrow eyes. "You're smart kids, all right," he said grudgingly. "Yes, Clara knew about the secret panel. Tonight we hid in the stairway behind it after we put the cassette player on in the tower room. But when you discovered the trapdoor behind the tower stairs, we had to hurry out and get back to the tower room without being seen.

"To get rid of Mrs. Montero and Andrés so that we could go up the main stairs, we set Pinky loose to run over those piano keys. We knew they would come to the performance room to investigate. Then we could slip out the rear door of the room and down the hall to the stairs."

Enrique sobered and mopped his face with a handkerchief. "But Luisa was upstairs prowling around. Clara panicked and hid herself somewhere, and I ran up the stairs to frighten Luisa with my disguise. When you kids saw me on top of the stairs, I turned to come down to frighten you, too, but you came after me."

He slumped back, his hands hanging limp over the arms of his chair. "That's all there is to tell," he muttered. "You know the rest. Now I'd like to leave."

Andy sprang out of his chair. "Just a minute, Mr. Cavallo. Don't you think we should find Clara first?"

They all looked at Enrique, who shook his head. "How should I know where she is? Probably did some disappearing act she remembered from Don Ramon's performances."

His words made Sara look up suddenly. *Disappearing act!*

Leaping to her feet, she cried, "I think I know where Clara is. But I'll need your help, Andy."

109

13

Like Old Times

WITH Andy falling into step behind her, Sara hurried out of the room and into the hall. She stopped in front of the knight's armor and whispered, "Open it, Andy."

The puzzled boy reached around the back of the armor and pulled it open. But this time the suit was not empty. A furious Clara Cavallo stepped out, looking at them angrily.

"So this is where you hid!" exclaimed Andy. Turning to Sara, he asked, "How did you know Clara had hidden here?"

Sara replied, "I didn't really know. But when Mr. Cavallo said that Clara probably did a disappearing act she remembered from Don Ramon's performances, I thought she may have hidden in the suit of armor near the stairs."

Without a word Clara Cavallo turned sharply toward the back door at the far end of the hall. Andy moved quickly in front of her. "You'd better come with us," he said, steering her away from the door. "We're all waiting for you in the parlor."

When they ushered the woman into the parlor, Luisa cried out, "Clara!" Then in the next breath she exclaimed, "What have you done to your beautiful long, dark hair?"

Sara thought that was a silly thing to ask just now. Then she saw Andy staring with surprise at the tall woman with the short red hair.

"So that's why I didn't recognize you that day on the pier, Clara," he exclaimed. "And yet I thought I had seen you before."

Clara Cavallo regarded Andy coolly. "At the pier I was afraid that you would. You see, I cut my hair and what was left I dyed red, so no one in Bayport would recognize me."

With a dry laugh, Clara turned and acknowledged Andy's mother. "I believe I have surprised even you, Dolores."

"You certainly have, Clara," Mrs. Montero replied. "But the reason why you're here surprises me even more."

In a disapproving voice she went on, "Smuggling ancient art objects out of Mexico is a terrible thing. They belong to that country and are part of its heritage. I believe the Mexican government has a law that priceless artifacts are not to be removed from their country."

Clara turned away, her face flushed with indignation. Her eyes rested accusingly on her husband. "Enrique, you talk too much. Come, I will not stay in this villa a moment longer." And with an angry toss of her head, she marched dramatically from the room with her sullen husband in her wake.

Andy started after them, but his mother motioned him back. Nobody in the parlor moved until they heard the front door click shut, then Mrs. Montero leaned back in her chair and said, "Thank goodness they're gone."

"Shouldn't we call the police or something?" Andy protested. "After all, Mom, you yourself said that smuggling is a terrible thing."

"They won't get far," Mike said, moving quickly out of his chair. "Not after I call the coast guard."

"The telephone is in the hall," Mrs. Montero told him.

While Mike dialed the number, Luisa clasped her hands together, looking greatly relieved. "Now Doña Dolores and Andrés will live happily in this villa without any more ghosts."

"And you will live here with us, Luisa, as long as you like," Mrs. Montero told her. "After all, you were to inherit the villa, too, and I know how much you love it."

Andy walked over to the housekeeper and sat down beside her. "I have a confession to make, Luisa," he said. "I thought you were behind all this at first. I—I guess it's because you were acting so secretive and didn't want us in the tower room."

Luisa leaned over and patted his hand. "I knew that something was going on up there the minute I stepped into the house," she explained. "That's why I didn't want you to have the key, Andrés, until I had time to climb to the tower room and find out for myself. But I have been so busy helping your mother get the villa in order that I had no time to go up there.

"Then the night when those strange sounds came from the tower and the ghost appeared on the stairs, I admit that I was too frightened to investigate. But tonight I thought I'd hide in the linen closet upstairs and keep watch in the hallway to see what was going on."

She paused, then turned to the five young people from Bayport. "I know how unfriendly I must have seemed, but I was not sure you weren't up to tricks. I knew how the young people of Bayport talked about the villa being haunted, and I was not sure of your intentions when Andrés invited you here. Will you all forgive me for my rudeness?"

Sam gave the housekeeper a tilted grin. "Of course, Luisa. How could we not forgive anyone who bakes such a scrumptious chocolate cake as you do?"

They all laughed and were still laughing when Mike came back from the phone.

"Mrs. Montero, I got the coast guard," he said. "The captain would like to talk to you."

While his mother was on the phone, Andy said with a happy sigh, "Well, now that the mystery is solved, I'm starved. I suggest we all go to the kitchen for some lemonade and the rest of that delicious cake."

"And then I go to bed," the housekeeper added. She glanced down at her wristwatch with a shocked expression. "Good heavens, it's twelve o'clock!"

* * *

The next morning at breakfast Andy came into the dining room with the white rabbit in his arms. He announced, "The Cavallos made off so fast last night that they forgot to take Pinky with them."

"Where did you find that rabbit?" his mother asked.

"Underneath my bed," Andy told her with a grin. "May I keep it, Mom?"

Mrs. Montero nodded with a sigh. "Yes, I suppose so, but not in the house. Pinky broke one valuable vase already."

"I'll make a bigger hutch for it out by the fountain," Andy said.

Pinky wiggled his nose at them all, but this time it made no attempt to leap from Andy's arms.

Lee ran her hand down Pinky's soft white fur. "What happened to Clara and Enrique Cavallo?" she asked. "Did the coast guard catch up with them?"

"The captain called about an hour ago to inform us that the *Sea Breeze* was sighted this morning on its way down the coast," Mrs. Montero replied. "It couldn't outrun the coastguard launch, and Clara and Enrique were soon caught and arrested. Captain Henderson said they told him the name of the smuggler they worked for in Mexico and promised never to take part in smuggling again. I suppose they hope that when the Mexican government hears that, their sentences will be lighter."

"What about the stolen art treasures?" Sam asked.

"The coast guard found the other cabin cruiser with the smuggled goods after Clara and Enrique were taken into custody," Mrs. Montero said. "The art objects are being returned to customs officers in Mexico."

"Wow! So the stolen goods arrived last night!" Mike exclaimed. "It was a good thing you asked us to spend the night here, Andy. We fouled up the smugglers just in time."

A happy smile lit Andy's face. "We sure did."

Mrs. Montero took a sip of coffee. She placed the cup in its saucer with a little clatter and smiled gratefully at the young people. "I can't thank you enough for what you have done for us," she told them. "I only wish Andrés and I could do something in return."

The five members of the youth group looked at one another knowingly and beamed.

Brian spoke up in an eager voice, "Well, you see, Mrs. Montero, we have this youth group at church, and every year we used to come here to the key for a cookout. . . ."

He broke off as Mrs. Montero said, "Yes, Andrés told me about your youth group. I think it would be fun if you have your cookout here on the key."

"Oh, wow, that's great!" cried Brian, clapping his hand over Andy's shoulder. "Will you come to the cookout, Andy?"

"Sure," replied Andy, "and maybe I can talk Mom into going to your church next Sunday."

Sara looked blissfully across the table at Andy. "That would be nice, Andy," she said.

"There is one thing, though, that Mom and I insist on," Andy added. He looked at them with sober, brown eyes. "Let everyone in Bayport know that the Spanish castle isn't haunted."

"We'll let 'em know all right," Mike promised.

After a little pause, Mrs. Montero said, "Luisa, Andy, and I are going to live here on the key. Since we cannot afford the upkeep of such a large house, we have decided to make a guest house out of the villa. The performance room itself can be made into several guest rooms, and I am sure Mr. Thomas can arrange a loan from the bank to help us with the renovation. It will be good to see happy families here, enjoying the key as much as we do."

"That's a wonderful idea!" Sara exclaimed.

"And no longer will this villa be called the Spanish castle," Andy announced. "From now on it will be called the Don Ramon Guest House." He turned to his mother with a sudden, concerned look. "Do you think Uncle Ramon would approve?"

"I think he would like that very much," Mrs. Montero said, smiling.

After breakfast as they were walking across the beach in their swimsuits, Andy pulled Sara aside. "Will you be my date for the cookout, Sara?" he asked.

"We don't couple up, Andy. It wouldn't be fair to the kids who don't have dates, so we all go as a group. But you can sit with me at the campfire. You'll have a lot of fun and I know the other kids will think you're just great."

Andy's face brightened. "You're pretty special yourself, Sara." Then, flushing, he ran for the surf. Sara felt her own cheeks grow pink with pleasure as she watched him go.

Sam, Lee, and Mike joined Andy, but Brian lingered on the beach.

"How about jogging one lap around the key before we swim, Sara?" he called to her.

"Okay, you're on!" Sara called back, running to catch up with him.

As they jogged side by side along the sandy beach, Brian said, "Hey, this is just like old times, isn't it?"

Sara looked out over the gulf to the sandbar where Andy waved a splash at her. She waved back. "It sure is, Brian," she answered. "Only this summer it's going to be even more fun."

And smiling to herself, Sara knew they wouldn't need to have another mystery to solve to make it that way, either.

The Author

Ruth Nulton Moore was born in Easton, Pennsylvania, and now lives in Bethlehem, Pennsylvania, with her husband, Carl, a professor emeritus at Lehigh University. They have two sons and five grandchildren.

A former schoolteacher, Mrs. Moore has written for children's magazines and is author of seventeen juveniles. *Danger in the Pines* won Christian School's C. S. Lewis Silver Medallion, and *In Search of*

Liberty received the Silver Angel Award from Religion in Media. Her books have been translated into Swedish, Finnish, German, Spanish, and Norwegian.

Mrs. Moore is a member of Children's Authors and Illustrators of Philadelphia, and her biography appears in *Contemporary Authors, The International Authors and Writers Who's Who,* and *Pennsylvania Women in History.*

When she is not at her typewriter, she is busy lecturing about her art of writing to students in the public schools and colleges in her area.

She belongs to Christ Church, United Church of Christ, and has been a Sunday school teacher.